Body of Water

The Wronged Women's Co-operative: Book 9

T E SCOTT

Copyright © 2024 T E Scott

All rights reserved.

ISBN: 9798328986090

Prologue

June 25th, 1994

"Can we listen to *Wet Wet Wet* again? I fancy that Marti Pellow," Bernie Paterson said, applying another layer of blue eyeshadow.

"Nah, it's depressing," her older sister Martha replied. "Put on that other tape, the one with *East 17* on it."

For once, Bernie didn't argue. If it had been one of her younger sisters, then she would have fought over the choice of song. But Martha was just home from college for the weekend, Martha had the best taste in music and Martha was *cool*.

The pop tunes filled the room as the tiny speakers on Bernie's second-hand hi-fi worked as hard as they could. It was Bernie's eighteenth birthday and Martha had turned up on the doorstep that afternoon with an overnight bag and a set of curling tongs.

"We're going out," Martha had said, dragging her sister upstairs. "And no argument about it. You're much too boring these days. It's your eighteenth birthday and we need to go dancing."

Bernie had been looking forward to a frozen pizza dinner and a lazy night watching old VHSs with her other sisters, but she could hardly say that to Martha.

"Where's the best club these days?" Martha asked. "Is it still the Zone on Sneddon Street?"

Bernie shrugged. "They're all bit crap," she said, trying to cover up the fact that she had never been to any. Unlike her friends with fake IDs who had been going out since they hit sixteen, Bernie had always had too many responsibilities. It wasn't fun to go out drinking on a Saturday night when you had two jobs to work on the Sunday. Bernie took a gulp of the Midori that Martha had found at the back of their mother's drinks cupboard.

"Did you see about that footballer going missing?" Martha asked.

As if Bernie could have missed it. The papers had been full of nothing else this week. "Footballer? For about five seconds. He was a joiner, worked at the care home sometimes. He went missing over a week ago, but no one gave a crap until they worked out he used to play for Invergryff Town."

"Did you know him, then?" Martha asked, her eyes wide.

"A bit," Bernie said. In fact, she had only met Gavin Eyre a couple of times and never spoken to him much, but she wanted Martha to be impressed. "Seen him around, that sort of thing."

"What do you reckon happened to him? Give me those

eyelash curlers, you look like a panda."

Bernie allowed her sister to do something frightening to her eyes. "I've got a few theories. His brother runs a pub called the Corner Bells over on the north side of Invergryff. A rough place, one of those with no windows. So you could be looking at a gang thing or –"

Martha burst out laughing. "I knew you would be all over this. Just like when you were wee and you were obsessed with Columbo and Quincy and who was the guy in the wheelchair?"

"Ironside."

"God, what a terrible show that was. You used to make us all watch them when they came on Channel Four."

Bernie took another mouthful of sweet liquid, but it seemed to have lost its effect. "What's your point?"

"Don't get snippy with me," Martha told her. "I just meant you love all that nosing about in other people's business, don't you? Finding out their nasty little secrets. And you can't help doing it in real life too."

"Aye, like your little secret for turning up here all of a sudden," Bernie snapped at her, fed up with holding her tongue.

"What do you mean? I came over for your birthday?"

"With a bottle that you bought from the local garage on the way here. I can see the price sticker. That means that it was a last minute trip. And your eyes are all red under your makeup. You've been crying. You broke up with that stupid boyfriend of yours, didn't you?"

Martha sniffed. "So sharp you'll cut yourself, aren't you Bernie?"

"Always."

There was a moment where no one spoke.

"My eyes aren't that puffy are they?" Martha asked, checking herself in the mirror.

Bernie tried to salvage the situation. "No, you look cute. Your hair is lovely."

"Thanks. I ironed it this morning. I'll do yours if you like?"

"No thanks. Remember when Deborah tried to do it once and burnt all along my ear? I've never done it since."

"Stupid cow," Martha said and they both started giggling.

"Yeah, she is. Sorry you broke up with… what was his name again?"

"Alan," Martha said, flicking a cotton pad into the bin. "Don't be sorry. He was a prick. Tell me about this bloke who's gone missing."

"Really?"

"Sure."

Bernie tapped her badly painted nails on the dressing table. "I reckon it's all to do with the brother. Either he is the killer, or he knows who is."

"You think the lad's dead then?"

"Aren't they always?"

Martha shivered. "I don't understand why you like all this dark stuff. Gives me the creeps. But I suppose it's harmless enough for you to talk about it. It's not like you can do anything, without being a cop or something."

Bernie shut her mouth. "Yeah, that's right." She looked in the mirror and wasn't too happy with what looked back at her. Make-up was a foreign country for Bernie. She had told Martha that she wanted to look like that Toyah Willcox, but she was a bit worried that she looked more like a Mr Potato Head who had visited the wrong part of town. And her clothes weren't quite right either. As a larger girl, Bernie had always favoured black, but the batwing top and the cheap gold jewellery borrowed from her mother's drawers made her look like she was going to a funeral, not a nightclub.

"I'm not sure we should go out," Bernie said. "I mean, you look stunning and I look like your fat pal that you've brought along to hold your drink while you go dancing."

"Oh come on now, it's Invergryff, not LA," Martha elbowed her in the ribs. "You'll be the hottest one in the room just because you've still got all of your own teeth."

Bernie couldn't help but laugh at that one. "I suppose so."

By nine o'clock they had said goodbye to the younger girls and made their way into town.

"This is the place your pal recommended?" Martha said when they had reached the bar, her expression bemused. "Jesus Bernie, it looks like the Krays would come here on their day off."

"My friend said that they had a great jukebox," Bernie replied, grabbing her sister's arm and pulling her forward. "And the drinks are dead cheap."

The second part of that statement was certainly true, Bernie thought when they had both bought their vodka sodas and retreated to a corner of the bar. It was just a shame that the place didn't seem to have anything else going for it. The barman had stared at Martha's chest the whole time they had ordered and the rest of the people there were either angry-drunk or sleepy-drunk and nothing in between. The floor and the tables were competing for a 'most sticky' award and the music playlist didn't seem to have anything recorded since Elvis died.

"Not my idea of a great pub," Martha said, grimacing as she looked around at the regulars. "Christ, that man's eating fish and chips out of newspaper on the bar. Why did you bring us here again?"

"Two drinks for a quid?" Bernie reminded her.

Martha pretended not to hear. "Do you think anyone would give me a ciggie?"

"You said you'd given up?" Bernie hated smoking. In fact, the grey fug that floated around the ceiling of their current location was already making her throat tighten.

"Aye, well, I say a lot of things," Martha said. She went up to the bar to order another round. Bernie took the opportunity to assess her surroundings. The pub was certainly rough, but there didn't seem to be any signs of trouble right now. There didn't seem to be anyone dealing either, although they might just be being discrete. Gangs? Well, that was a possibility. There was certainly an unfortunate range of knuckle tattoos on show, but Bernie was out of her depth where those things were concerned.

"I got us doubles this time," Martha said as she put the glasses down. "And a guy at the bar gave me a ciggie. He's about eighty and only has one eye but I reckon I might be in there."

"Sounds lovely," Bernie said. She noticed a muscular figure appear through a back door behind the bar.

"Hey, you're not even listening to me, are you?" Martha pouted.

"Of course I am," she replied, wondering if the man might turn around so she could see… yes, that was him all right.

"That's the brother," Bernie hissed, unable to keep her thoughts to herself. "Francis Eyre. Doesn't look like he's heartbroken about Gavin's disappearance, does he?"

"Hang on a sec," Martha put down her drink. "That's why we're in this dump, isn't it? Good jukebox my arse. I should have known, they've had Status Quo on three times already. You only came here so you could do your wee Hardy Boys impression."

"If anything I'm Nancy Drew," Bernie said, unmoved.

"This is how you want to spend your eighteenth? Stalking some poor soul whose brother has disappeared."

"Better than getting drunk and snogging some lad with frosted tips while dancing to Mariah Carey."

Martha threw her head back and laughed. "That doesn't sound bad to me at all. Come on, let's finish our drinks and get out of this hell-hole."

While Martha chattered away, Bernie couldn't take her eyes off Gavin Eyre's brother. He was a large bloke, with a thick neck and hair shaved close to his skull. He looked like the sort of person who would steal your purse and then give you a kicking, just for the hell of it.

"Wait here a sec," Bernie said to Martha, ignoring her sister's complaints as she walked over to the bar. She made sure to stand on the right-hand side where Francis was serving.

"All right lass, what can I get you?"

Bernie smiled. "It's my eighteenth birthday today."

"Happy Birthday," Francis said, not bothering to look up from the bar where he was cleaning a glass.

"How about a free drink?"

The man laughed, a wheezy sound that suggested he was a smoker.

"What do you think I am, a charity?"

Bernie shrugged. "Worth a try. Can I get two vodkas and soda then please?"

She took a deep breath as Francis poured the drinks. "I don't suppose there's been any news about your brother?"

The glasses clanked down on the counter. "Naw. What's it to you?"

"I knew him a wee bit," Bernie said, ignoring the man's glare. "I work in the care home and he used to come in and do odd jobs. He hasn't turned up then?"

"It would be in the papers if he had, wouldn't it?" Francis replied.

"It must be such a worry for you all," she said.

"That's one pound twenty." Francis held out his hand.

Bernie gave him the money. "What do you think happened to him?"

"No idea," Francis said. He flung the coins into the till and then stomped away down the other end of the bar.

"You should mind your own business, darling," a man at the bar with a Celtic shirt on and seriously bad BO told her. Bernie turned and walked back to her table.

"You weren't harassing that guy were you?" Martha asked when she sat down.

"Just asking some questions," Bernie replied.

"Jesus Bernie, you don't think you've got enough on your plate what with working full time and looking after everyone now that our mother's scarpered? Why are you getting involved in this?"

Bernie struggled to explain. "It's just… what if I could help? The police don't give a crap about it, you can tell from their faces. If there's something I can do, then don't I owe it to his family?"

"Isn't he his family?" Martha said, dipping her head in the direction of the brother.

"I don't mean that guy. I mean the mother. Didn't you see her on the news? Barely able to speak, grey skin, eyes red… The sort of grief I see all the time at the care home, but this time it's a young guy that's dead and that's just not right."

"But why you?"

Bernie didn't reply. If Martha couldn't understand then how could she explain it? Didn't her sister feel that low-level rage when she saw an injustice being done? Didn't everyone?

Martha took a swig of her vodka. "I want to go dancing. Look, why don't I have a wee chat with your pal over there? If he admits beating his brother to death with a claw-hammer then we can go out clubbing, right?"

"It's not a joke, Martha," Bernie warned her. "Just look at the guy. I don't think you should be messing about with him."

"But you can, is that right?" Martha narrowed her eyes. "Don't see why I'm not allowed to give it a shot."

Bernie was worried that Martha had drunk more than she realised, but she couldn't stop her sister from marching over to the bar. She followed behind her and sat down on a stool where she was blocked from view by a pillar.

Martha was already chatting to Francis, flicking her hair back and pouting her lips as she talked. To Bernie's immense irritation, it seemed to be working and the man was even smiling at Martha, showing his nicotine-stained teeth.

Bernie zoned out while Martha made small talk with the man for a few moments, then tuned back in when her sister got to the matter at hand.

"I always try and catch an Invergryff Town match when I'm at home," Martha said and Bernie had to choke down a laugh at the lie. Martha couldn't care less about football. "I don't suppose they're playing on Saturday?"

"Nah, it's an away match."

"Your brother was a footballer, wasn't he?" she asked, fluttering her eyelids again.

"He… yeah, he was." Francis's smile had disappeared. "How did you know that?"

"Oh, it was in the papers."

Bernie knew before the man stepped back that they were in trouble.

"I see." Francis looked around, then his face turned red as he noticed Bernie.

"Oi, you," he said to her. "I suppose this girl is another nosy mate of yours."

Bernie said nothing.

The man turned back to her sister. "You can get out of my pub. You and your fat friend."

Martha hissed in a breath, glancing at Bernie to see if she had noticed. She had.

"Wouldn't want to stay in this dump anyway," Martha said.

At that moment Francis took a step towards them and for a moment Bernie thought he might actually hit her sister. The veins on his forehead were popping out and the muscles were tense around his neck. She raised her own arms in protection when a shout went up at the other end of the bar and there was a sound of smashed glass.

"Christ!" Francis pushed past them to the pile of bodies where someone was already holding up a broken bottle as a weapon.

While this was going on, Bernie allowed Martha to lead them over to the other side of the room.

"Look, I'm happy to give him a piece of my mind," Martha said. "Once he's finished pulling those guys off each other."

"Don't worry. I'll take care of it."

"All right, I'm going to nip to the loo before we go." Her sister gave her a sharp look, despite the double vodkas. "You're not going to cause any trouble are you?"

"Wouldn't dream of it."

"Good."

Bernie waited until Martha turned her back, then she walked back over to the bar. She checked that her sister was still in the loos, then she walked towards the brawl. She waited until the men had stopped punching each other and everything had gone quiet. Then she kneed Francis Eyre in the nuts.

Chapter 1: Mary

Mary Plunkett was readying her house for visitors. This was a long process that generally took at least a day. When people arrived at her home she always said 'sorry for the mess', knowing fine well that if they could see how messy it normally was, they would have gone straight back out of the door again.

She pushed her thumbnail under a tube of toothpaste that had somehow become attached to the gas fire and yanked it off. She dropped it in the bin bag next to the coat-hangers that had been twisted into swords and a multitude of odd socks whose partners would never be found. Mary looked around the room for any further signs of slovenliness. Just about messy enough for normal people, she thought. Time to put the kettle on.

Three minutes early, the bell rang. Mary put down her mug of tea and went to the door which was already open.

"I thought I'd let myself in," Bernie Paterson said, chucking her coat over the banister. "Can you pour me a big glass of water? I'm just back from the gym and I'm parched."

"Of course," Mary said, hurrying to comply. Their private investigation agency, the Wronged Women's Co-operative, was supposedly run as a partnership. But Bernie Paterson was definitely the one in charge. Even though she had been working for her for two years now, Mary still hadn't got over her Bernie fear. The woman was tough in more ways than Mary could imagine. Whereas she was, and would always be, a wet lettuce.

It wasn't an official WWC meeting tonight, just an opportunity for Mary and Bernie to go over a recent case. Still, Mary had sent the kids to their grandmother's for the night. They had a bad habit of making faces at Bernie behind her back and stuffing wet tissue into her shoes.

Besides, Mary had a funny feeling that she was about to get a bollocking, and that wasn't something she wanted the kids to witness.

Bernie took out her laptop and sat down on the sofa, indicating that the small talk was over and it was time to get to business. Mary sat down opposite her on the uncomfortable armchair that the kids had squished most of the stuffing out of.

"All right, let's go over the Anderson case. I want to work out what the hell went wrong."

Mary squirmed, and not just because someone had left a pencil sharpener embedded in the creases of the armchair.

"Why couldn't Liz make it again?" She asked, wishing the third member of their team was there to provide a buffer from Bernie.

"Hair appointment. Besides, the Anderson case was all yours, wasn't it?"

"Yes," Mary said miserably. "It was all mine."

"Take me through it from the start," Bernie said, her fingers poised over the keys like she was about to take down a statement in court.

"I guess I should have realised it was going to be a disaster from the start," Mary said, tugging at her hoodie so that it stretched over her curled-up form. "Niall Anderson was one of those guys who thought he knew what our results were going to be before we had even started."

"It was information on his boss he wanted, is that right?"

"Yeah. Anderson was due to attend a disciplinary hearing next week. He was accused of inappropriate behaviour at a staff night out. Not groping some poor woman, for once, but for leaking company secrets."

Bernie nodded her head, her fingers flying over the laptop keys. "What line of business were they in again?"

"Haulage. You wouldn't think it's the sort of business that people are spying on one another, but apparently some of the tenders can be worth tens of millions of pounds. This staff night out was an industry awards evening, the sort of thing where they charge you a hundred quid for a ticket and then give you some bullshit award like 'Year's shiniest truck' or something."

"Keep to the point," Bernie said, reminding Mary of every teacher she had ever had.

"Right. At this event it wasn't just Anderson's company, there were representatives from all the main haulage contractors across the UK. And when one of the Edinburgh firms wins a tender a week later, with a remit that sounded very much like the one Anderson had put together, his employer started to get suspicious."

"Sounds like a tricky one to prove."

"Aye, but some of the wording in this Edinburgh-based company's documents was identical to the ones Anderson produced, so it doesn't look good for him. But Anderson swears blind it wasn't him. He reckons that one of the other staff members got drunk and blurted it out to the wrong person."

"Even harder to prove," Bernie said, shaking her head.

"Exactly. But we had one thing in our favour. The venue where they held the event managed to give us full CCTV of the entire evening. They always have it for these things because so many people nick stuff from the tables."

"And what did the CCTV show?"

"That Anderson never went near anyone from the Edinburgh team. Morningside Trucking, they're called. And that seemed to be all we had, until I found footage of a blond woman that wasn't on the staff list snogging the head of Morningside Trucking in the corridor outside the event."

"And you decided to show this footage to Anderson."

"Yes," Mary said, her face flushing with embarrassment at the memory. "It was a mistake. A big mistake. What I hadn't realised, you see, was that the blond woman was Anderson's wife. And she was passing information onto Morningside Trucking because she was shagging the boss. Anderson hadn't realised either, until he saw the footage."

"And what happened next?"

Mary shuddered. "It was just my luck that at that moment the wife came in. Anderson lunged for her and... well, I couldn't let him beat her up, could I? So I tripped him up as he went past and he went crashing through the glass coffee table."

"Four stitches and a broken rib," Bernie said, checking her notes. "And what did the wife do?"

"She legged it, heading off in his brand new Audi. I had to wait until the ambulance came. That was an awkward twenty minutes, I can tell you."

Bernie pinched the bridge of her nose. "And now he's refusing to pay."

"Yep. Says we owe him for the Audi, and the money his wife took out of their joint account. It's all got a bit... heated."

"Right, well from what I can see you made one big mistake."

"I should have checked out who the woman was first," Mary said, nodding her head.

"Well, yes, obviously you should have done that. But a bigger mistake was not getting the final payment up front."

"Noted."

Bernie sighed. "I'll pop around and see this Anderson character. We completed the job as promised: it's not our fault that he didn't like the outcome."

If anyone could persuade Anderson to part with his cash it was Bernie. Mary was pleased that she hadn't been given too much of telling off. Bernie could be reasonable sometimes. It was almost as unsettling as when she was a nightmare.

"Did you see the commotion over at the reservoir today?" Mary asked, now that Bernie had closed the laptop and gone to grab her coat.

"No," Bernie said, "I've been in the gym all afternoon. Working on my glutes." She did a disturbing squatting motion so that Mary could admire the muscles in question.

"Well, they look... nice," Mary said, shaking her head to remove the image. "I was driving past the woods up on the South Brae today and there were a whole load of police cars parked up at the reservoir."

"Really?"

"Yeah. And there was a works van there too, along with a small crane."

Bernie frowned. "That is strange. One cop car I could understand if they're doing work, but several? Did you check the grapevine?"

"Of course," Mary smiled. The grapevine was their name for the various strands of social media that were this decade's version of village gossip. "There were several messages about it on the Invergryff Crowd page. Apparently they were emptying the reservoir today."

Bernie tilted her head to the side. "But... would that need a load of cop cars?"

"Exactly what I thought," Mary said, nodding in agreement. "But at first I wasn't too sure what to do about it. I mean, with Walker away, it's not like I can just find out what's going on at the station. But then I kept coming back to the crane. And I wondered if it was the one operated by Amber Bellingham's husband."

"It was?" Bernie was already grinning.

"Yep. And you know how Amber loves a gossip. She told me that the reason there was such a fuss up there was that they had found a bunch of abandoned cars once they drained all the water out. And in one of those cars they found a body."

Bernie's eyebrows arched. "Now that is very interesting."

"Apparently it's been in there a long time. Amber said it was pretty much a skeleton and that the whole thing had been 'well gross'."

"I bet it was, if it's been there that long." Bernie hitched in a breath and stopped on her way to the door. "Hang on, tell me again, when was the car from?"

"Mid-nineties they said."

Bernie stood up so suddenly that she sloshed coffee onto the table. "I knew it!"

"Knew what?"

"Everything. Get me the police on the phone. It's time to say

'I told you so'."

Chapter 2: Walker

Sergeant Owen Walker couldn't believe his luck. After two weeks of his own personal hell, working his way through the syllabus for the National Investigator's Examination and learning more laws and jargon than he ever thought possible, he was being allowed out on the streets. He hadn't exactly regretted his choice to join the plain clothes officers while he had been sifting through endless training documents, but he was definitely glad to be out in the fresh air and away from the words that always seemed to dance their way across his screen.

"You reckon you'll pass the exam then?" Sergeant Rav Sangar paused from drinking his coffee to field the question Walker's way.

Rav was ten years younger than Walker, good looking and brilliant with spreadsheets. Walker was trying his best not to hate the man's guts.

"Exams are not exactly my strong point," Walker told him. There wasn't much point in pretending otherwise. Despite being one of the oldest officers there, he was always the slowest to do the reading. He just had to hope that his general knowledge and experience made up for it.

"I'm sure you'll smash it," Rav said, with the confidence of a man who had never been sent to the bottom group for spelling.

"I'm looking forward to today," Walker said, changing the

subject. "We're shadowing a family liaison officer, right?"

"Right. We're meant to be there in half an hour, want to grab breakfast first?"

Another thing that was irritating about Rav was that he was always eating and never putting on weight. As they headed over to the canteen in the basement of the police college, Walker promised himself to avoid the bacon rolls for once. He was enjoying having access to a proper breakfast, unlike the overworked vending machines back in Invergryff station. He grabbed an instant porridge bowl and tried not to watch as Rav attacked his plate of bacon, black pudding, eggs and square sausage with glee.

"I barely slept last night," Rav said, grabbing his cup of coffee and draining it. "The walls in this place must be made of paper. I hope it wasn't you snoring like a hippopotamus."

"I don't snore," Walker lied. He might well have been the perpetrator as his recent co-habitation with Mary Plunkett had made him capable of sleeping through anything. Constant yelling and giggling by primary aged children had made him immune to noise. Sleeping in the police college with no one trying to shove raisins up his nose was borderline heavenly.

"Have you met the family liaison officer before?" Rav asked.

Walker shook his head. "It's DS McNicholl, isn't it? I've heard she's a stickler for the rules, but she knows her stuff."

"Makes sense. You want to be on the right side of the police code when you've just told someone their loved one's dead, right?"

"Right," Walker agreed.

Rav shovelled some beans onto his fork. "Don't get me wrong, I'm looking forward to being on the ground for a bit, but I don't think Family Liaison work will be for me."

"No?"

"Too much tea and sympathy," he shuddered. "What about you, where do you want to specialise?"

"Violent crime," Walker answered without hesitation. "I want to be on the Major Investigation Team for unlawful deaths. What about you?"

"Counter-terrorism," Rav said. "With this brown face, I reckon I'm a dead cert."

Walker laughed at that. "You think because you're Asian they're going to recruit you?"

"Definitely. I can go undercover as your nastiest Bin Laden type. You'll see."

"Aren't you a Sikh?"

Rav punched his arm. "Aye, but the terrorists don't know that. I'm hoping for a move down south at some point. I've always fancied living in London."

"I'd rather stay up here," Walker replied.

"You won't get a choice though, will you? That's the thing

about SCD, they can send us anywhere."

"Right," Walker said, trying not to think about it. The idea of being away from Invergryff would have been appealing a few years ago. But now that he had made a life with Mary and her kids, it wasn't quite so easy.

Rav checked his watch. "Better get going. Is it in reception that we're meeting McNicholl?"

"Aye." They walked quickly through the college, even though it was a bit of a maze. Tulliallan was a Victorian castle that had been co-opted into service as the training building for Police Scotland. It was universally known as Castle Grayskull, due to its uncanny resemblance to the home of the eighties favourite cartoon hunk, He-Man. Mary had actually squealed with joy when Walker had shown her a picture.

Waiting in reception was a female officer with dark black hair that had a streak of grey at the front and cool blue eyes.

"Owen Walker and Ravinder Sangar?"

"Just Rav," the man said.

"And you go by Walker, is that right?" DS McNicholl said.

"That's right," Walker replied. He wondered if she was going to ask why, but the woman was already walking towards the door.

"You can call me Gill," she said, gesturing for them to follow her. "I want to get going. I didn't realise I was going to be bringing trainees along today."

Rav and Walker glanced at one another. Her tone told them that she wasn't too happy about the idea.

"But I guess you'll see what it's really like to work in the front line with vulnerable family members. I want your complete focus and no mistakes."

Walker swallowed and managed a nod.

"Who wants to drive?"

Rav took the wheel and Walker squeezed into the back of the car while McNicholl sat in front of him. He tried to pretend that the faux leather seat wasn't covered in crumbs and slightly damp.

"It's a bit of a weird one today," McNicholl said once they were on the motorway. "We don't have a definite ID yet on our victim, so normally we wouldn't be speaking to the family straightaway. But this is an old case, one that is well known to the public, so we want to give them a courtesy call." The woman made sure they were paying attention, carefully wording the last sentence. "The last thing we want is for them to learn about it on the news."

Both Walker and Rav nodded in agreement. Every police officer understood that they were often in an unacknowledged race against the media when it came to information. Especially in the days of the camera phone when the news didn't even have to wait for the papers to be printed.

"I think we're heading to your neck of the woods, Walker," the DS said. "You stay in Invergryff, don't you?"

"Been there for a couple of years now," Walker replied, his interest growing. "Is that where we're off to today?"

She nodded. "Yes. We're going to catch up with a family that is known to the police, for a variety of criminal activities. But today we're bringing them bad news and I want you two to stay well back."

"Why?"

"Because it might get nasty," the DS said, her brows lowered. "And I don't want to have to write a report on why I got two trainee detectives in a whole heap of trouble."

"You think there will be trouble then?"

McNicholl shrugged. "You see people under strain in this job. They lash out. That's when you need to fall back on your training, make sure you behave to the letter of the law."

"Who did you say the victim was?" Walked asked her.

"No definite ID yet, remember," she chided him with a tight smile. "But we're letting the family of Gavin Eyre know about the discovery of human remains. The dates fit with his disappearance thirty years ago. And some items of clothing may be a match, but we're not letting them know that yet. Not until the techs have had a good look at them. What's the station like?"

Walker knew this was a loaded question, but he tried to answer as honestly as he could. "The Superintendent is MacKinnon and he's a good bloke. Firm but fair. Very experienced. There's no Detective Inspector stationed there since DI

Macleod went on medical leave, so I'm not sure who they will make Senior Investigative Officer."

"They'll send in a Major Incident Team most likely. A DI at the least."

"Think we'll be able to get involved?" Walker asked.

McNicholl turned to face him. "Well, you're meant to be training with me for a week so as long as I'm part of the case then you will be. But once I have to move on, you'll be back at the college. Don't you have the NIE coming up?"

"Don't remind me," Walker groaned.

"I guess Rav here will be okay," she continued. "Didn't you score top of your year when you first joined the force?"

Rav gave a chuckle. "Yeah, so they tell me."

"Bet you'll sail through the exam then," McNicholl replied.

In the back of the car, Walker tried not to think about smacking Rav across the back of his head.

Chapter 3: Bernie

"I'm not sure that a thirty year old case is worthy of an emergency WWC meeting," Liz said, dropping into the seat opposite Bernie. They were in Mary's house which was not Bernie's favourite choice for a WWC meeting. But when she had heard the news of the body found in the reservoir, Bernie hadn't wanted to wait around to change venue.

"You're just grumpy because you had to cancel your hair appointment," she said as Mary handed out the drinks.

"Riri's the only woman in Invergryff who knows how to cut black hair, so yes, I am annoyed. It'll take me weeks to book her in again."

"All right," Bernie said, trying to move the conversation on, "but I've just learned that a case that I thought was dead has come back to life."

"Zombie-style," Mary nodded. "Just like in the movies."

Bernie ignored her. "Anyway, I've spent all day chasing up the details. I'm ninety-nine per cent sure that the body they've found will be identified as Gavin Eyre."

"The name sounds familiar," Liz said.

"It should do. It was big news at the time. Mainly because Gavin had played a bit for the local football team when he was younger so they had plenty of pictures for the paper. Nineteen ninety-four. Seems like a lifetime ago."

"Oh aye, that was the year that it rained all summer," Liz said. "I was sitting my exams and it just felt bloody miserable. Trying to work out what Lewis Grassic Gibbon was on about for my English higher. All those fields and horses and miserable, grimy kitchens."

"Ugh, I studied that too, Sunset Song, wasn't it?" Mary said. "Too much farming and too little snogging as far as I was concerned."

Bernie cleared her throat. "Let's return to the important subject, shall we? Summer of ninety-four when a young guy disappeared. And now we're going to solve his murder."

"Are you sure it was murder?" Mary asked.

"What else would it be?" Bernie snapped back. "You reckon he drove himself into the reservoir? Waited in the car while it filled with water? Hell of a way to commit suicide. Much easier to down a bunch of pills and a bottle of vodka."

"Could it have been an accident?" Mary continued. "I mean, the car could have swerved off the road or something."

It was Liz's turn to tackle this one. "Not possible. We should go up to the reservoir and show you one day, but it's not somewhere you would drive into by accident. You have to take the car through a gate in a fence, then down a footpath. You couldn't end up there unless it was on purpose."

"It's just the sort of place where you would dump a body," Bernie said. "Which makes it even more ridiculous that those idiots at the police station never thought to check there."

"Maybe they did," Liz shrugged. "It's a huge area. It sounds like they would never have found them if they hadn't emptied all the water out."

"The perfect place to hide a body," Mary said and Bernie had to agree.

"At first no one seemed to care that he'd gone missing," she explained, taking a sip of her gin and tonic. "Then someone realised that he used to be a footballer. A minor one, only played in one professional season, but that was enough to get him on the news. Pro footballer disappears, that's what the headlines said."

"And they never found any trace of him?" Mary asked.

"Nope. Don't you remember? They said it was a mystery, like he was abducted by aliens or something. You must have seen it in the papers."

"I was ten," Mary shrugged. "I think that was my pony phase. All I wanted to do was watch Black Beauty and pretend I owned a horse. They even let me ride one from the local stables for a bit."

Bernie rolled her eyes. "Of course you were one of those horsey girls. I bet you stuck rosettes up on your wall."

"Would have done if I'd ever won any," Mary explained. "I fell off the first time and broke my wrist in two places. Never got on a horse again."

"That's a shame," Liz said.

"Aye, a real tragedy," Bernie snapped back. "Unlike that poor bloke that got murdered and dumped in a reservoir. Now let's have a think about what we're going to do about him."

"What about the family?" Liz asked. "Are they still around?"

"Yeah, that's where we're going to start. The dad died a while ago. Reggie, I think that was his name. But the mum and the brother are still alive. The brother though…" Bernie shook her head. "He's a right piece of work."

"What do you mean?"

"He used to own a pub back in the day, and a rough one at that. I had to leg it out of there one time because I… Well, it doesn't matter now. I saw him a couple of years ago and he's the sort of guy you would cross the street if you saw him coming. He's got a scar from ear to ear and about four teeth. He looks like an extra from *Peaky Blinders*."

"Could he be a suspect?" Mary asked. "I mean, brothers fight don't they? Wouldn't be the first time that it ended in murder."

"He'll go on our list," Bernie replied. "But I remember at the time I never found any definite evidence that he was out to get his own brother. He even tried to get the police to reopen the case a few times over the years, but nothing ever came of it. Blokes like Gavin disappear and no one cares."

"You cared though didn't you Berns," Liz said, giving her a sharp look.

"What do you mean?"

"Well, you knew all the details of this as soon as it came up. You knew the family, all about the victim. You were just eighteen, but you remembered all about it."

Bernie allowed herself a smile. "Do you know, I never thought about it before but I reckon you're right. It was the first time that I realised that the coppers can't solve every crime. And that pissed me off. And I wasn't able to do anything about it, and that pissed me off more. But now I'm finally in a position where I can do something. And I fully intend to do it."

Chapter 4: Liz

Liz was waiting for Mary to turn up in the local garden centre. Liz had no interest in gardening, but it was one of Mary's favourite places to grab a cuppa, mainly because it had scones the size of her head. For her part, Liz was determined to avoid the temptation of baked goods. It was turning out to be a lot more difficult to lose the baby weight in her forties than it had been the first time she was pregnant.

She grabbed a latte and dragged over a high chair for Issy. As she wedged her chubby legs into the chair, Liz realised that it wouldn't be long before her daughter was too big to fit in a high chair. Just another little milestone that crept up on you when you weren't looking. She provided Issy with the buttered toast she had bought and her daughter began to fling it around the room quite happily. Considering she couldn't put on her own shoes, Issy had quite the throwing arm.

"Sorry for the mess," Liz said when Mary arrived, clutching a plate heaped with cream and jam.

"Don't worry about it. Think she'd like a bit of scone?"

Mary held out her offering to Issy who grabbed it and shovelled it into her mouth.

"She's just the cutest," Mary said.

"When she wants to be," Liz said with a slight sigh. "I'd forgotten how much work they are at this age."

"Yeah," Mary gave her a sympathetic smile. "Old enough to get into mischief but not old enough to care about getting told off."

"Exactly. Let me get a wipe for her face."

Liz pulled out her Mulberry black leather handbag. When she was still working at the accounting firm it had been pristine, and incredibly expensive. Probably best not to think about how it was now covered in nappy cream and leftover biscuit crumbs.

"What do you think of this new case," Mary asked once Liz had removed some of the sticky residue from her daughter's face.

"I think it's going to be a lot of work," Liz said, her forehead wrinkling. "I mean, there's no point in arguing about it, but I don't think it's going to be quite the walk in the park that Bernie reckons it'll be. It was thirty years ago, for a start. Bernie might have taken some notes, but she was an eighteen year old kid, not a private investigator."

"It's weird to think of Bernie as a teenager," Mary said. "Did you know her back then?"

"No. It wasn't until later that we met."

Issy gurgled and chucked a crust at an old man on a neighbouring table.

"You're a couple of years younger than her, aren't you?" Mary asked.

"Yeah, I was only sixteen when Gavin Eyre went missing," Liz told her. "I can only barely remember it. I was sitting exams at the time and that was basically the only thing that I thought about."

"You were a swot?"

"Totally. I mean, it wasn't that I was super clever or anything, but I wanted to do something important." She shrugged. "And something that earned decent money. It wasn't like mum and dad were poor or anything, but it wasn't always easy for them finding work back then. A lot of folk took one look at them and showed them the door."

"I guess black faces stood out a bit more in ninety-four," Mary commented.

"You're not wrong. It was still true when I went to uni. I was the only black girl in the class. Don't get me wrong, I owned it, but it might have been nice to have someone to talk to that understood how it was."

"Hopefully things will be different for Sean," Mary said. "I mean, I know that the school is a lot more diverse than when I was a kid."

"True," Liz said, although she wasn't always quite so optimistic. Now that Sean was hurtling towards adulthood she worried about his status as a black kid in a white town more than she ever had. But that wasn't something that Mary Plunkett could ever understand, even though she could tell the woman was trying. She went back to the easier subject of unsolved murder.

"One problem we're going to have is doing research," Liz said. "So little was online by that point that we're not going to find it quite so easy."

Mary nodded. "I was thinking about that. A lot of newspapers have been digitised now, but it's the social media stuff we're missing. It's amazing to think there was a time before every idiot in the place could post their own idle gossip."

"Yeah. I think we'll try speaking to some of the journalists that wrote the articles at the time. Find out what they couldn't put in their official stories."

"Good idea."

"Thirty years ago," Liz shook her head. "In information terms, it might as well be a hundred years ago. We've been spoilt in the last few years. I'm not sure the WWC would even have been able to exist back then."

"With Bernie around it would have," Mary grinned.

"Yeah, that's true." Liz looked at Mary's nearly empty plate and tried not to think about how much she wanted to eat like that herself. "Wouldn't mind having my sixteen year old figure, mind you."

"I used to think I was fat when I was sixteen," Mary said. "Remember it was all 'heroin chic' by the time I hit my teens. Now I would kill to have that stomach."

"I think I peaked in my twenties," Liz said, smiling at the memory. "Short skirts and high heels. I would fall on my arse if I tried that now."

"I bet you were a bombshell," Mary said.

"I did go out a fair bit. I was single for all of my twenties, so it was definitely party time."

"Really? I met Matt when I was twenty-one."

Liz couldn't think of anything worse than being coupled up so young. "I didn't meet Dave until I was nearly thirty."

"You were single for ten years?"

Liz didn't like the other woman's tone. "Yeah, so?"

"It's just surprising. I mean, look at you, you're gorgeous!"

"Well, that's clearly true," Liz laughed. "I guess I just never found anyone worth settling for, you know? Not until I met Dave. Plus I was more interested in my career."

"I never cared about my career," Mary said with a shrug. "I mean, I did my degree course in biology because it was one subject I was okay at when I was at school. Then I fell into the job with the environmental company. But I always wanted to be a mum."

"Did you really?" Liz had never really thought too much about being a mother before it actually happened. She was happy about it, of course, but she found Mary's approach to life baffling.

"Yep. And Matt seemed like the sort of guy that would make a good father. And to be fair, he wasn't terrible until the whole 'stealing all our money and gambling it away' thing."

"That was a bit of a shocker, right?"

Mary tucked a hair away from her forehead. "In hindsight, not so much. Like I said, we were young when we got together and he was one of those guys that never really grew up. The gambling was something he did with his mates in the pub. And then when they all got older and his mates stopped going to the pub all the time, it was something he did by himself. And I guess that's when it went from a hobby to a problem. But you know I can't hate him for it. If we hadn't got together I wouldn't have had the kids."

Liz wasn't so sure she would be as pragmatic about it, but Mary was a gentle soul. She had never seen her friend shout or even lose her rag at the kids, even under extreme provocation like when her oldest boy 'borrowed' the neighbours jet washer.

"What's the plan for this case then," Mary said, licking a spot of cream from her knife.

"Bernie's working it out just now. She wants to talk to the police first, of course. I don't suppose Walker would be able to help?"

"Nah, he's in Tulliallan all week. There's this big exam they have to sit to meet the requirements for SCD. He's terrified, not that he would admit it."

"Because of the dyslexia thing?"

Mary nodded. "Aye. It's funny really. My Peter was only six when we realised he had a problem with his letters. The school got him a diagnosis pretty quickly and he's never looked back. But Walker went through his whole time at school with everyone just telling him he was thick. That sort of thing leaves a scar. If he just keeps his cool, he'll ace the exam. But it's the fear of looking stupid that's holding him back."

"You miss him a lot then?" Liz probed. Mary and Walker's relationship was a continual source of fascination for her. She'd never quite worked out how they managed it, with conflicting careers and four kids to navigate.

"I do," Mary's smile was a little forced. "But he's wanted to move to plain clothes for years. If us being apart for a few months is what it takes, then I'll just have to get on with it."

Issy squealed and demanded to be lifted out of the chair.

"That's my cue to leave," Liz said, wrestling her daughter into the buggy.

"I never got a chance to ask you if you'd had any luck tracing the Hart family," Mary said as they were walking towards the car park.

Liz pulled a face. "God, that is the case from hell. No wonder Bernie dumped it on me as quickly as she could." Elspeth Hart had died last year and they had been trying to find any living heirs that might inherit her not inconsiderable fortune. Liz quite enjoyed this sort of work normally, working out family trees and so on. But the Hart's had been a promiscuous bunch, with multiple marriages and children born out of wedlock. It was taking more hours than they would ever make back in their fees.

"Bloody nightmare," Liz added when explaining this to Mary.

"You'll find them," the other woman said with a cheerful confidence. "You're brilliant at that sort of stuff.

"Am I?"

"Yep. You're the clever one. I'm the wet lettuce and Bernie…

Liz laughed. "Bernie's the one that haunts your dreams."

"Aye."

Chapter 5: Mary

By the time the kids got back from school Mary's lovely quiet tea with Liz was long forgotten. She had decided to do some life-admin and it was not going well. Twice a year or so, she got all the kids to put on their shoes and trainers and see what still fitted, but Mary was already regretting this burst of organisation.

"How can every single one of you have grown out of your trainers at once?" Mary asked, staring down at her children who were pulling off the offending shoes. "And Peter, I only bought your ones a couple of months ago. What the hell happened?"

"You're always telling us to eat healthy so I grow big and strong," her son told her. "I guess it worked."

"Well, it's junk food and candy from now on," Mary told them.

"Really?" Four happy faces looked up at her.

"No, not really you wee monsters," Mary said, grabbing them in for a hug. "Now go upstairs and pretend to be ninjas."

"Really? We can fight?"

Mary laughed. "I meant because they're silent. But if you can kill each other without making a noise then go ahead."

She checked her watch. Walker was meant to call any minute, so she hurried to the kitchen to make a cup of tea. Since he had moved over to Tulliallan for Specialist Crime Division training she had come to treasure every moment they had together, even if it was just a few words over the phone.

Just as she was about to sit down with her cuppa she remembered that she was behind on the washing. She moved out to the lean-to utility room and started to shove clothes around in an attempt to get organised.

At that moment her phone rang.

"Are you all right?" Walker said once she had answered the call. "You sound out of breath."

"Just dealing with the washing mountain," Mary said, huffing and puffing as she loaded the tumble dryer. "Please tell me about your day. It's got to be more exciting than shaking the mud off football socks."

Walker laughed. "Would you believe me if I say I missed that washing pile?"

"No," Mary replied. "I live here and I would happily burn it to the ground. Go on, tell me about some police stuff."

"All right. Well, we've started shadowing the Family Liaison Officer today."

"God, that must be a hard job," Mary said.

"Aye, but it's interesting. And you get to help people when they really need you."

"You'll be good at that," Mary said loyally. "After all, you took us lot on."

She enjoyed the sound of Walker's laugh down the phone. "Oh, I'm sure you'd have been fine without me. You haven't found someone else to watch your Star Trek box sets with yet?"

Was he jealous? Mary thought it was quite sweet. "Not yet. Are you still coming home on Sunday?"

"If I can. I might manage to see you this week though."

"Really?"

"Yes. I've been assigned to a case in Invergryff," Walker explained. "It's a suspicious death from years ago but they've only just discovered the body. I don't suppose…"

"Oh, that'll be the Gavin Eyre case," Mary replied, shoving as much school uniform as she could into the already full washing machine. "Bernie's all over it. Do you know she tried to investigate it back in 1994?"

"Of course she did," Walker said. He didn't sound too pleased.

"It's not going to cause you any problems, is it? The WWC being involved I mean."

"No more than usual."

Mary tried to think of a way to lighten the mood. "It's the kids' sports day next week and both Lauren and Johnny have come down with mysterious illnesses that only affect their ankles."

"I'm sorry I can't make it," Walker said.

"Oh it's fine, I mean I wasn't expecting…" Mary bit her lip. "I just meant it's funny because they hate sports and they always make up some stupid excuse to get out of it."

"Right."

Mary tried not to let her sigh be audible down the phoneline. The truth was that Walker felt worse about him being away than she did. Mary was used to being a single parent, and while having a handsome, funny and brilliant boyfriend was lovely, she didn't depend on him to make her life easier. Maybe in the future she would, but at the moment she was coping with their current separation surprisingly well.

"I'd better go," Walker said. "You will try and keep Bernie Paterson in check on this one, won't you?"

"I'll do my best," Mary said, knowing that she wouldn't. Part of Bernie's brilliance was her ability to take on anyone. No matter what Walker wanted, Mary had to admit if there was ever a question about her irritating the police, she would be team Bernie.

Mary put her phone back in her pocket, not too happy about how the conversation had gone. Somehow, she never got the chance to tell Walker that she did miss him. That even with so much of her attention being occupied with four tiny people and their constant demands, there was a part of her heart reserved just for him. She just had to hope he wasn't having too much fun while he was away.

"Vikki's upstairs in a mood," Peter said as he stomped into the living room. Since his move to High School her son seemed to occupy more space than before.

"What did you do to her?" Mary asked wearily.

"Nothing! Well, I did call her penguin-face, but she was already upset before that."

"Penguin face?"

"Because her lips are like this," Peter demonstrated by pulling his own lips out in a strange beak-like motion."

"Right. Well, don't call her names, okay? Why don't you go play outside for a bit while I talk to her."

"Good luck," Peter shook his head. "Women."

Mary decided not to rise to the bait and merely rolled her eyes at him. She made her way upstairs to find that Vikki had curled up on Mary's bed. She didn't blame the girl. The house that they were living in only had three bedrooms, which meant that Vikki had to share with her five year old little sister. It wasn't an ideal living arrangement, but that was what happened when you divorced your gambling addicted husband. The alternative would have been worse, she told herself, even though it didn't always feel that way.

"What's up love," Mary said, sitting on the bed next to her daughter.

"Peter is a a-hole," Vikki grunted, her face in the pillow.

Mary took a deep breath. "Firstly, we don't call our brothers names. And secondly it would be 'an a-hole' not 'a a-hole'. Grammar is important."

She had hoped that might earn her a laugh, but Vikki just shrugged.

"You know that he's just playing up for the sake of it," Mary explained. "It's nothing to do with you. I'll have a word with him about his behaviour. Again."

Vikki pulled her face from the pillow. "It's not just him."

"Okay," Mary said, waiting quietly.

Eventually the words came out in a flood. "It's sports day this week and I hate all sports and I don't want to come last. All the other girls are good at sports and their hair is much nicer than mine and they all like better music than me and… ugh." Vikki buried her head back in the pillow.

"Ugh," Mary said in agreement. She stroked her daughter's hair until her breathing slowed a little. "And do you think everyone else is just confident about all this stuff? I don't suppose that Nia is feeling like this? Or that Chloe Brown is worried about tripping over her shoelaces? Or that girl who always wears a Taylor Swift t-shirt is scared of coming last?"

"Her name is Sophie and she has three dogs."

"Does she now?" Mary hid a smile. "So you don't think that Sophie with the three dogs is worrying about Sports Day too?"

Vikki's eyes peeked over the cushion. "No…"

"Well, I'll tell you something for nothing. Everyone worries about things like this. No one wants to look like an idiot in front of their friends, whether it's for tripping up in the race or having a terrible hair-do or… Did I ever tell you about the time my mum gave me a perm when I was fourteen?"

"Like a million times."

"Well, it's a deep-seated trauma," Mary said, squeezing her daughter's shoulder. "Look, I can't tell you that you're going to go out there and win every race. But I can tell you that it's perfectly normal to feel nervous and worried about everyone looking at you. But here's the thing: everyone is too worried about themselves to be looking at anyone else."

"They are?"

"Yep."

"I bet Peter doesn't think like that."

"Maybe not. But Peter thought it was a good idea to put a pack of crayons through the tumble dryer so let's not look to your brother for the best examples of what to do, right?"

"Right," Vikki sniffed, but her expression had lifted a little. "You know he said I look like a penguin."

"He's being ridiculous," Mary said, pulling her in for a cuddle. "You're much more like a beautiful parrot, or a wise owl, or maybe one of those birds that eviscerate people with their talons. Yeah, one of them."

"You're so silly, mum," Vikki said, but she squeezed right

back.

Chapter 6: Walker

It was their second attempt to speak to Francis Eyre and Walker could tell that DS McNicholl was feeling nervous. Her fingers were drumming the steering wheel as they waited outside the man's flat.

"I hope this goes better than it did with the mother," McNicholl said, her eyes flicking to the doorway. Mrs Eyre had barely said two words to them during the visit. A carer had been in looking after her and despite McNicholl's assurances that they were there to help, the police officers had met a frosty reception. Her son was dead, Mrs Eyre had told them. She didn't need a body to tell her that.

"I guess they're not the sort of family who are going to open up to a police officer," Walker said.

"Nope. There's a history there. The father, Reggie Eyre, he was a big deal back in the seventies. Clever, never got caught for much but did some time for supply. We reckon he was part of a big drugs ring, but not the head guy. That was a Glasgow gangster. All long dead now."

"And did the brothers go into the family business?" Rav asked.

She shrugged. "You've read the file on Francis Eyre?"

Both men nodded. Walker had caught up with the case files the night before. Not everything was digitised, of course, which made things a little trickier, but there was plenty of information on Francis Eyre in the last few years.

"Francis strikes me as a low-level habitual criminal," he said, watching McNicholl's face to see if he was on the right track. "He's done time, mainly when he was younger, a bit of GBH and dealing. Not so much in the last few years but that bar of his has featured in plenty of assault reports."

"That's right," McNicholl nodded and Walker was pleased he had done his research. "Now, there's a couple of ways that Francis's background might be relevant to the case. Firstly, it gives us some idea of the sort of people the Eyre brothers were associating with at the time. And secondly, it suggests that we need to consider Francis as a suspect."

"Is there any evidence to suggest that the brothers had fallen out?" Rav asked.

"There might be something in the original witness statements. We're working on getting them all uploaded from the archives at the moment. But we could really do with taking a statement from the man himself."

It was another twenty minutes before a hunched figure appeared around the corner and made his way towards the block of flats. DS McNicholl jumped out of the car and the other two followed behind her.

"Francis Eyre?"

A suspicious set of eyes swivelled towards them. Eyre looked older than his years with a broad back which had hunched in on itself. When he spoke Walker could see he was missing a few teeth. That and the scars on his face suggested that the man had not lived a quiet life.

"I'm busy," Francis said as they walked up to him. "I don't have time to chat to the cops."

"I'm DS McNicholl, these are Sergeants Sangar and Walker. Could we have a word with you inside?"

"Mum already called," Francis said, making no move to let them in. "She said you haven't got a definite ID yet."

"That's true. We're waiting on the DNA results. But it's looking like the human remains we found might fit the description of your brother." McNicholl tilted her head to one side. "Are you sure you wouldn't prefer to have this conversation inside rather than in front of the neighbours?"

Francis shrugged. "Fine. But wipe your feet on the way in."

Walker realised this was ironic when he walked inside and saw the state of the man's hallway. Not only could it do with a good clean, it was full to the brim with stuff.

"I do some bulk selling," Francis said when he saw them looking at the cardboard boxes stacked up to the ceiling. "All bought legitimately before you start."

"We're not here to look into your business practises," McNicholl said as Eyre led them into the living room. The only items in the room were a black leather sofa and a huge telly which told Walker that the man was probably single.

"Nice setup," Walker said when he noticed the gaming PC

connected to the telly. "Is that a flight simulator you've got over there."

"Aye, and that's bought out of my own money and all," Francis said.

"I like a bit of flightsim myself," Walker explained. "I run it on an ultra wide monitor."

"Nice. What sort of stick?" Francis asked.

"A VKB Gladiator." Walker said. "But I had the same as you before. Thought about going VR?"

"Nah, I'm old school," Francis replied.

McNicholl gave Walker a look and cleared her throat. "We would like to have a chat about Gavin if that's all right, Mr Eyre. I know it is a difficult time for you."

"Naw, thirty years ago it was difficult. Now it's just... bloody depressing."

"We were hoping you could confirm the description you gave of Gavin the last time you saw him before he disappeared," McNicholl said, opening up her notepad. "You told officers at the time that he was wearing blue jeans, a black hooded top and a white t-shirt."

"If that's what I said then it must be true," Eyre replied.

"You haven't had any ideas since?"

"No. That was meant to be your job, wasn't it?" Eyre sniffed. "You know I tried to get them to reopen the case. Only last year I was down at that station, asking them to look into some people that might have had it in for him."

"We have your statement from last year," McNicholl said. "Is this the complete list of names of people you think could have been involved."

She brought up a screen on her tablet.

"Aye, that's it. Filed it away in the bin, did they?"

"Not at all. I can see from the files that each of these names was investigated. Two of them have died since ninety-four. The others didn't seem to have any connection to your brother going missing."

"How would you know after all this time?" Francis Eyre said and Walker had to admit he had a point. There was a reason that historic crimes like this one often remained unsolved.

"It is a challenge, Mr Eyre. But there is a good chance that if these remains do turn out to be your brother's then we will have enough new physical evidence to get to the bottom of what happened to him."

Francis shrugged and stared out of the window. Walker was finding his attitude puzzling. On the one hand he had hassled the police to look into his brother's disappearance, but on the other he just seemed to want them out of his house.

"Is that everything? Coz I've got to get back to the pub."

"Can you just take us through the last night you saw your brother?"

The man tugged at his nose. "Fine. It was April nineteenth, he came into the bar for a couple of drinks. He said he was working the next day, but didn't say where."

"He was a joiner, is that right?"

"Aye, and a general handyman. He'd been doing a lot of work in the care home so I assumed that was where he meant."

McNicholl checked her screen. "But he didn't turn up to the care home on the twentieth?"

"No. Of course, I only found that out on the day after."

"The twenty-first?"

"Yes. My mum called me to say he hadn't come home. At first we thought he'd just stayed out that night. It wasn't like now when everyone had a mobile phone. I just thought he was staying at a mate's house or something."

"And you gave the police a list of his mates?"

"At the time, yes, for all the good it did me. When he didn't come home that night either, I told Mum to go to the police station."

"And that would be the missing person's report made on the twenty-second of April."

"If that's what your paperwork says, then it must be true," Francis said with a humourless grin. "But when I started chatting to his mates it turned out no one had seen him since that night in the pub. So he'd already been missing three days."

Walker said nothing, but he could see that the old anger still lingered in Eyre. The thing was, unless there were definite signs of foul play, an adult going missing was never going to be any officer's priority. It wasn't like Gavin had been considered vulnerable, or that they had proof something bad had happened to him.

"What do you think happened, back in ninety-four," Walker asked the man.

"I think that Gavin got into something he shouldn't have. And I think someone killed him for it. And seeing as he's been rotting away in the reservoir for all these years, it looks like I was right."

They didn't get much more out of the man after that. McNicholl left her card, but Francis just chucked it onto the coffee table. The mood in the team was not too perky when they left the flat and got back in the car.

"Where now boss," Rav asked, turning the key in the ignition.

"We're heading back to Tulliallan," McNicholl said. "And you two need to write up what we did today for your assignment. Try and make it sound like it wasn't a total wash-out."

Walker's heart sank. "Ah, I thought we might be staying here tonight."

"Afraid not. I've got paperwork to fill in and you lot have some studying to do I'm sure. Besides, until we get the ID on our victim, there's not much a Family Liaison can do right now."

McNicholl's phone rang before the car had moved.

"Hold off a second, let me take this." She got out of the car and Rav flicked the engine back off again.

"You were hoping to see the Missus, is that right?" Rav asked while they waited for McNicholl to return.

"Yeah, but she'll understand," Walker replied, hoping it was true. Unlike previous girlfriends, Mary had never complained about the hours he was forced to keep, but even she had to have a limit.

"Is it three kids she's got?"

"Four."

"Wow, she lucked out didn't she?" Rav laughed.

"Meaning?" Walker's voice was tight.

"Come on mate, she's a single mum with four kids, she must have thought her lottery ticket came in when she hooked up with you."

Walker felt his hands twitch into fists and was going to reply when his phone buzzed. He glanced down and saw that Mary was sending him a Doctor Who meme where the Doctor was regenerating into Taylor Swift for some reason.

"I'm the one that's lucky," he said to Rav. "And if you met her you'd understand why."

"All right mate, don't get your knickers in a twist," the other man said.

Walker bit down on a retort. He reckoned Rav was one more disparaging remark about Mary away from getting his head kicked in.

Chapter 7: Bernie

It was far too hot in Invergryff police station, especially for Bernie Paterson who had just been to the gym for a spin class. She fanned herself with a leaflet about human trafficking.

"You can't put the aircon on, can you?" Bernie asked.

"You joking?" The constable at the reception desk snorted a laugh. "This building was built in nineteen sixty-three. No air conditioning, no lifts and barely any flushing toilets."

"Just as it should be," Bernie nodded. "Keep the copper's egos in check."

The constable's smiling face fell and he turned back to his computer screen where Bernie was fairly certain the man was playing Solitaire.

"Would you like to come upstairs, Mrs Paterson," a voice said from the doorway.

Bernie followed the man who had introduced himself as Sergeant Neil Michelson. Bernie recognised him from previous visits to the station. Solidly built, he had a round face and a Glasgow accent.

"I was hoping to speak to an inspector," Bernie told him as he took her into an interview room.

"I know," Michelson said. "Your request was noted. Unfortunately, none of our inspectors are available at the moment. You told reception that you had some information pertaining to a police matter."

"It's about your dead body from the reservoir. Gavin Eyre."

The man had a half decent poker face. His expression barely flickered at the name.

"I'm afraid we haven't confirmed the identity of –"

"What a load of rubbish. You know as well as I do who disappeared thirty years ago. And –"

"Hang on, I've got some notes for this meeting," the sergeant said, reaching into his pocket. Bernie was impressed that a police officer had actually done some work for one of their meetings.

"If any members of the WWC turn up," Michelson read from the piece of paper in his hand, "watch your back. Especially if it's Bernie Paterson."

Bernie narrowed her eyes. "What did you just say?"

"Just something a friend of mine gave me."

"You don't seem like you'd have many friends," Bernie snapped back.

"Don't pay any attention to Paterson's insults," Neil said, reading from the paper. "She thinks she knows everything."

"Just what sort of notes are these," Bernie said, folding her arms.

"Sergeant Walker gave me them. If it makes you feel better, he does add: quite often she knows something, but never as much as she thinks she does."

"I'm going to have a word with that man," Bernie replied.

"Oh, he said you would say that too. And he's put a note here that says: 'You can tell Bernie Paterson that I've warned every person in the station that she's not to take any liberties while I'm away.'"

"Huh. I wonder what he means by liberties?"

"Possibly requesting an interview with a senior officer on an active murder investigation when they might be kind of busy?" the Sergeant suggested. Bernie was starting to go off the man.

"I'm sure Walker would remind you that I never waste anyone's time, not least my own," she told him. "I wouldn't have come here if I didn't have information critical to the investigation."

"All right," Michelson snorted a laugh. "Let's hear it."

Bernie pulled out a pile of photocopies from her bag. "You better be careful with these," she said as she pushed them across the table. "I've still got the originals, but I used up half of Liz's printer ink to make the copy."

"What are they?"

"My original investigation notes."

Michelson glanced at the pile of paper. "Sorry, are you saying you were a private investigator back in ninety-four?"

"Not exactly. More of an interested amateur."

"Is there any actual evidence in here?" Mickelson was flipping through the pages in a derisory way. "All I can see is a load of newspaper clippings and handwritten notes."

"It's everything I worked out at the time. A list of suspects, a timeline of the victim's movements…"

"All based on supposition?"

"Based on what the locals told me at the time," Bernie said. "I would imagine it's a hell of a lot more accurate than their memories are going to be nowadays, thirty years down the line."

"Ah, I see you have a whole section of files named 'Police Incompetence'," the sergeant reminded her.

In hindsight, even Bernie could see that it might have been better to leave those out.

"I got the impression at the time that the police thought the lad had just run off. Moved away, gone to London or something. If it hadn't been for the football angle it probably wouldn't even have made the newspapers."

Michelson leaned back in his chair. "So why were you so convinced that something had happened to him."

Bernie thought back to her earlier self. The Bernie with the plus size jeans and the equally large need to prove herself. It was hard to imagine she had ever been that girl. "I guess it was the family dynamic. There was something a bit off about the brother, and I'm not just talking about his criminal record. I always felt that he knew more than he was letting on."

"You interviewed Francis Eyre at the time?"

"In a manner of speaking," Bernie replied. She didn't need to bother the man with the details. "He was a local character, you might say. And that pub of his was an absolute dive."

"We are aware of the family's previous interactions with the police."

"A crooked bunch the whole lot of them," Bernie agreed.

Michelson's neck was growing red. "Look, it's not that I'm not grateful for any information you can give us, but we will be conducting our own investigation."

"You'll start with Gavin Eyre's disappearance, right?"

The man sighed, "Like I said, we're not even sure of the identity of the body."

"Ha!"

"And I would respectfully request that you do not start any speculation until it has been released."

"And when will that be?"

"They can't announce the name until there's a formal identification," Mickelson said.

"That'll take a while won't it," Bernie said tapping a finger against the table. "Wouldn't think there's much more than a skeleton left of the poor bugger. Or was it like one of those bog bodies, perfectly preserved under the mud."

"Couldn't say."

"But you do think it'll be announced soon," Bernie said, stroking her chin. "Which means that you must have found something more than just the body. An identifier of some kind."

The police officer had their lips pressed together.

"Now it wouldn't be a wedding ring as he wasn't married," Bernie continued. "And probably not anything like a mobile phone as there weren't many of them about in ninety-four. So maybe a wallet of some kind?"

"I can't confirm a thing," Mickelson said. "Have you finished yet?"

"I'm just getting started. Have you informed the brother yet? You know that he moved to Paris, right?"

Mickelson frowned. "Paris? But he's…"

"Ha, Paris my arse. I just made that up to see your reaction. You have informed him, then, and you know that he's still living in Invergryff. Maybe I should go and speak to him myself."

"You better bloody not," the sergeant said, his face turning a darker shade of red. "Look, I shouldn't be telling you a god damn thing, but if you must know we're confirming with the DNA lab today and if it's a match, we'll be sending the family liaison out to inform them this afternoon. I think they'd rather hear it from us rather than some middle-aged busybody."

Bernie nodded. "Of course. I would never want to interfere with police process. What on earth do you take me for?"

Mickelson just raised his hand and pointed to the door.

"I can find my own way out," Bernie said sweetly.

"I'll accompany you to reception," the man said, holding up his notebook so that Bernie could read what was written and underlined three times. *Do not let Paterson walk through the station unattended. Last time I did that she found her way to the Super's office and started reading his private files.*

"I miss Walker," Bernie said as Mickelson led her out of the room. "He was the only one of you lot with any brains."

Chapter 8: Liz

Liz wasn't sure when she had become the official 'posh' one of the group. It obviously couldn't be Bernie: she was as working class as you came. If it wasn't for her hatred of carbs she would be a scotch pie. Mary was her own weird little class, definitely middle but with an eccentricity that meant she was also some sort of sprinkle-covered donut.

"And you're a pistachio éclair," Mary had told her when explaining her 'class wars through baking' system.

"You know my mum was a cleaner in a church, right?" Liz told her. "I'm not sure where you're getting the whole posh thing from."

"You look smart, you used to be an accountant and your hair is always perfect," Mary said with a nod of her head that had indicated the discussion was over.

This was why Liz had been sent to speak to the local paper. As the 'posh' one, the pistachio éclair, the others thought she might be more likely to get a result. After all, there was no reason why anyone would speak to them, even if there was still someone around from nineteen ninety-four.

The offices of the Invergryff Gazette used to take up an entire Victorian building on the north side of the river. Now they had been relegated to a couple of offices in the basement while the rest of the place had been sold off to nail salons and vape shops. There was probably some metaphor there for life if you looked hard enough.

"Can I help you?" A bored-looking girl in a headscarf and fake eyelashes was sat behind the reception desk.

"I rang up earlier. I've got a meeting with your senior editor."

If Liz was honest, when she had been told she was meeting the paper's oldest journalist, she had thought it would be a white-haired old man drinking whiskey he kept in his desk drawer. What she hadn't expected was an efficient-looking brunette in her fifties with a two-piece suit and a smartwatch.

"I'm Laney Blackwell," she said in a posh Edinburgh accent. "I heard you wanted to talk to me."

Liz nodded as Blackwell led her to a small office next to the marketing suite, which was much bigger and seemed to have several people working there.

"That's where the money is now," Blackwell explained when she saw where Liz was looking. "The stories are just a way of getting people to click on our ads. We've got two junior editors and me, and that's it for actually writing the stories now. They'd sack me if they didn't have to worry about how much redundancy I'd be in for."

That introduction out of the way, Blackwell offered Liz a smile. "But you don't care about any of that. You're here about Gavin Eyre."

"How did you guess," Liz said, perching on the plastic chair opposite the woman's desk.

"It's the only thing anyone can talk about. And when Gavin disappeared I was the one writing the stories, so of course you would come to me. Never thought I'd be writing that he had been found. Not after all this time. Still, it'll get me a nice little commission when the Nationals pick it up."

"You must have been quite young to be in charge of the story in ninety-four," Liz said.

"Flattery will get you everywhere," Blackwell said, her eyes twinkling with humour. "Yes, I was twenty-four and thought I knew everything, like you do at that age. I'd just finished my journalism degree at Napier and Invergryff was my first job, apart from a bit of freelancing here and there. I thought it was a bit of a backwater at first, but somehow I got used to it. In the big cities there's a lot more competition, but down here you can make a name for yourself."

Liz nodded. "Gavin Eyre was a big story for you."

"Damn right. Although we thought it was a bit of nothing at first. Despite what the general public believes when they're cosied up on the sofa at night, people go missing all the time. The stats tell us that 170,000 people a year in the UK just vanish."

"What?" Liz thought she must have misheard the number. "That can't be right."

"Believe me, I've done the research. In Scotland alone ninety people are reported missing every day."

"But that can't be true, surely."

Blackwell shrugged. "It only makes the news if they turn up dead. Or if they're kids, of course."

"So why did Gavin Eyre make the news?"

"He didn't at first. Just a small paragraph on page eight about a local lad gone missing. Then we realised that he used to play for Invergryff Town and that gave us an angle on it."

Liz made some notes. "Can you remember who it was that first brought your attention to the case? Did the police issue a statement or…"

"No, it was the brother. Frank or…"

"Francis," Liz prompted.

"Ah yes, that was him. I remember because he looked like a bit of a hardcase. Used to run one of the local pubs. He came in and told us his brother was in trouble."

"That was the way he phrased it?" Liz asked. "Not just missing but in trouble?"

Blackwell frowned. "Christ, it was thirty years ago, it's not like I can remember… But he did seem agitated. Worried. I can't be certain, but I was left with the impression that he thought something had happened to the lad."

"And you talked to the police?"

"Not that I learned much. I don't think they wasted much time looking for him. That was one of the things we went after, of course. Local cops don't have a clue, that sort of thing."

"And what about now? What's your angle for today's paper?"

"The police have just confirmed the ID, so we'll be going with the 'missing man's remains found in reservoir' for the paper, and for the tabloids it'll probably be 'horror find as body dug up from pond' or something similar. You have to pitch your stories to the appropriate market you see.

"Is there anything you know that wasn't in the paper back then," Liz asked. "You see, we're trying to find out what happened to him. For his mother's sake."

The other woman narrowed her eyes. "There's no point in making an appeal to my sympathetic side, you know. I've seen more weeping mothers than you've had manicures."

"There wasn't anything you kept off the record, then?" Liz prompted. "Anything unusual?"

"Not that I remember. I could look out my original notes for you. They're probably in some folder at home. If you're lucky they might even be word processed by that point in the nineties. I started off on an electronic typewriter, you know."

"That would be great, thank you."

"If I had to guess, I'd be looking at drugs. That pub his brother ran was dodgy as hell back then, everyone knew it. And it wouldn't be the first time some thug from Invergryff thought he was hard enough to tackle the Glasgow bosses. They get smacked down pretty damn quickly, that's for sure."

Liz picked up her bag. "Thank you for your time," she said, not that she had learned all that much.

Blackwell grabbed her sleeve. "And you'll give me an exclusive interview if you solve this before the cops, right?"

"What?" Liz said, startled.

"You didn't think I was giving up my time today for nothing, did you? Come on, it'll be great publicity for your agency. We can do a full two page spread, link to your website, all that marketing crap that the guys next door love."

"I guess we could work something out," Liz replied. There was no way she wanted her face plastered all over the local rag, but she could imagine Bernie would quite enjoy the publicity.

"Excellent," Blackwell replied and her smile now seemed like the sort that might meet an unsuspecting swimmer in the ocean. "I'll hold you to that."

Chapter 9: Mary

Her whole life, Mary had been cursed with being nice. It was a sort of mental affliction, like being scared of heights or forgetting people's names. Mary remembered everyone's names, sent them cards on their birthdays and always asked after their children. This was because she was nice.

Only Bernadette Paterson could find a reason to weaponize this quality.

"That's her place over there," Bernie said, pointing at a small white semi-detached building with paint flaking on the door. "She's pretty much housebound. I know one of her home carers, and she says that Elsie keeps to herself. Complains that her son never visits, poor thing. What she needs is someone to talk to. Someone to be –"

"Nice. I got it."

"Don't get that sour face on you," Bernie told her. "I've told you before, it's a bloody super power. I've never been called nice in my life."

"You surprise me," Mary replied.

"Now, while you're being nice to the woman make sure to find out if she has any idea who killed her son. Especially if it might have been Francis. If he hated his brother enough to kill him, then the mother will know that."

"Right. Ask the bereaved woman if her son committed fratricide. Anything else?"

"You know the drill," Bernie held up three fingers. "Suspects, motives, timeline. There are my notes of course, but we need to work on getting a firm sequence of events and that's not going to be all that easy after so much time has passed. So we'll need Mrs Eyre's help on that one."

"You think she'll be up to all this?"

Bernie shrugged. "The carers say she's a little withdrawn, but no dementia."

"Okay then," Mary said, running out of excuses. In truth, she was excited. After the disaster of the Anderson case, she needed to get her confidence back. Little old ladies always liked her, she found, and she was sure that Mrs Eyre would be no different.

With a final nod to Bernie, Mary got out of the car and made her way up to the front door. They had already learned from the carers that Elsie never went out in the afternoons, so even when the doorbell wasn't answered immediately, Mary knew to wait. A few minutes passed and Mary rang the bell again before a shadow appeared behind the half-glazed door.

"Yes?" The face was small and sharp, under short lank hair, with a wary expression. Of course, that was standard for someone with an unexpected arrival.

"I'm a private investigator," Mary said. "I was hoping I could have a quick word with you."

"About Gavin?"

"Yes."

Mary got ready to walk inside, just as Mrs Eyre slammed the door in her face.

She didn't need to look back at the car as she could hear Bernie laughing even though she was still on the front step. Channelling her inner Bernie, she put her finger back on the doorbell button.

This time, Mrs Eyre gave her a prize glare when she opened the door.

"I'll call the police, you know. That family liaison woman was here yesterday. I bet she'd like to hear that you vultures are sneaking around. Bloody paps. You lot killed Lady Di and all."

"I'm not a journalist," Mary said quickly. "I really am a private investigator. And my colleague has been looking into your son's case since nineteen ninety-four."

That made the woman pause. "Since Gavin disappeared?"

"Exactly."

"Why isn't your colleague here then?" Mrs Eyre said, her face still pinched with suspicion.

Mary couldn't exactly give her the true answer, which was that Bernie Paterson had been banned from speaking to anyone who might be considered vulnerable due to her tendency to tell them to buck up and stop being such wimps.

"She felt that I might be in a better position to speak to you today. I have two sons, and I can't imagine how awful it would be if one disappeared."

"No, you can't."

"But I can try to understand if you will talk to me." Mary felt the icy glare warm just a degree or two. "We're not the police, so we don't come at these cases with the usual prejudices. We take our time to learn about what really happened. And who Gavin was before he was taken from you."

That earned her a shrug. Mrs Eyre turned her back on Mary, but crucially the door was left ajar.

"Thank you," Mary said as she followed the woman into a small living room that smelled like reheated soup and had the sort of swirly carpet that hadn't been fashionable in decades.

Mrs Eyre seated herself on the sofa at the far wall. The curtains were drawn and the whole place made Mary feel like this was the sort of room you used to hide yourself away from the rest of the world. The TV flickered into life as the woman put on Bargain Hunt.

"You can have five minutes," she said, not looking up from the screen.

This would be what Bernie would describe as a 'hostile witness', which Mary reckoned she had learned watching bad American cop shows. In fact, Mary could see that what she was dealing with was a very frightened woman. Mrs Eyre's hands trembled on her lap and although she kept her eyes on the screen, she was tense with anticipation. But why was the woman so nervous? Surely the worst had already happened.

"It must have been difficult when the police told you they had found Gavin."

"They've been around here twice. First time they said they had found 'human remains' and they needed to check the DNA. But I knew fine well it was him before some laboratory confirmed it."

"Why was that?"

Mrs Eyre clicked her tongue. "Why do you think? A mother knows when her child is dead."

Mary wasn't too sure about that, but she kept her tongue.

"Do you have any pictures of him?" Mary asked as the other woman lapsed back into silence.

Mrs Eyre nodded and bent down to a sideboard next to her armchair. She pulled out a collection of old photographs in cheap frames. There was one of Gavin Eyre in a school photograph, one upper tooth missing and hair in a classic eighties bowl cut. Another had Gavin and Francis arm in arm, topless in the sunshine. They looked to be around six and twelve. And the last was of a teenager looking proud in a football uniform.

"We didn't take as many photos back then," Mrs Eyre said, as if apologising for the meagre collection. "This is the one that was in all the papers."

She handed over a photograph of a young man, again in a football shirt. His head was half turned away from the camera and he looked like he was about to laugh.

"It must have been terrible for you," Mary said, thinking of her own boys. "Especially not knowing what had happened to him."

"I always knew he was dead," Mrs Eyre said stiffly, repeating what she had told Mary earlier.

"Really?"

"If he'd been alive he'd have gotten in touch, wouldn't he? He wouldn't have left his mum worrying about him. No, by the end of the first week I knew he was never coming back."

Mary wondered if the woman was telling the truth. Wouldn't you always hope that your son was alive, even if logic told you otherwise? Mrs Eyre was so tightly wound it was hard to read her, but maybe that was just the way the woman showed her grief.

"Can you tell me about the last time you saw him?"

Mrs Eyre's eyes dropped and Mary had the feeling she was about to be lied to.

"It was April 19th. A Friday, it was. He came in late from the pub."

"He'd been drinking."

"A bit. He didn't seem too drunk. Not that I would have

blamed him. He was a young lad after all." Mrs Eyre's mouth moved like she was chewing a wasp. "Aye, that was the last I saw of him. He was meant to be working at the care home early, so I never thought twice when I got up and he had already left."

She stared at the screen again.

"It's never been as good since David Dickinson left," Mary commented.

"Aye, that's true. I miss his wee orange face."

"Me too," Mary said. She moved around so that she could see the screen. "They're not going to buy that silver tea set are they?"

Mrs Eyre nodded, her eyes lighting up. "They'll be lucky if they get twenty quid at auction for that."

"True." Mary sat down next to her. The woman flinched, but she didn't tell her to leave. "What do you think happened to Gavin?" Mary asked her softly.

"He was one of those boys that was always in the wrong place at the wrong time," Mrs Eyre said, her voice low. "If a group of lads were shoplifting, he'd be the one caught with the sweets in his pocket. Or the one to fall off his bike when the polis were chasing them. Everyone always goes on about my Francis and his troubles with the cops, but when they were younger it was Gavin that was always being brought home in the back of the panda car. But there was no badness to him, see? He just wanted the other boys to like him."

"That can be a dangerous trait," Mary said.

"Aye, you're not wrong. So I don't know exactly what happened to him. But I reckon he was doing someone else's dirty work, something like that. And then some evil bugger killed him."

It felt cruel to keep pushing what was clearly a painful topic for the woman, but Mary didn't have a choice if they wanted to find out the truth.

"And there was nothing different about him before he died? Nothing to suggest he might be in trouble."

Mrs Eyre's eyes stayed on the telly, but her hands fidgeted in her lap. "There might... He was spending a lot more time out of the house. You know what young lads are like. If he wasn't working then he used to mope about here, watching the telly and getting under my feet. But the couple of weeks before he... It's funny looking back, I thought he might be going steady with someone."

The old-fashioned phrase took Mary a minute to decode. "You mean he had a girlfriend?"

"Nothing serious, of course, or he would have told me about her. But I wondered if that was where he was going. And he seemed in a better mood somehow, like life was looking up for him. Hah! Should have known that's not how things work out, not for folk like us."

Mary took a deep breath, knowing that the next question would not go down well. "You mentioned that Francis has been in trouble with the police. Do you think he could have had anything to do with –"

"Out!" Mrs Eyre said, getting to her feet more quickly than Mary thought possible. "How dare you… Get out of my house."

Mary was out of the door before she could even see if the Red or Blue team had won. But at least she had learned something about why Mrs Eyre was so scared. The ferocity of her response to Mary asking about Francis had told her that his mother was terrified that he might have been involved in Gavin's death. The question was: was she right?

Chapter 10: Walker

The team had an early start to drive back to Invergryff from Tulliallan on Thursday morning, but Walker felt it was worth it to be back in an MIT briefing. Rav who had slept most of the way over, didn't seem quite so enthused.

"I prefer my crimes a bit fresher," he explained. "This case has nightmare written all over it."

If it weren't for the fact that he was back in Invergryff, Walker might have agreed. But along with meeting up with his colleagues and catching up on the station gossip, Walker was pleased to have another day away from the college and the threat of the upcoming exam.

"Can you two be quiet for a minute," McNicholl said from the back seat. The DS had turned up looking rather rough that morning.

"It was my sister's baby shower last night," McNicholl had explained. "All the babies and bumps and the bucket loads of oestrogen have given me a headache. The two bottles of wine might have had something to do with it too."

"Let me know if you need a cheeky spew in a layby," Walker had replied, earning him a decidedly un-baby friendly middle finger from the back.

Walker was enjoying the fact that McNicholl was loosening up around them. The DS seemed to view them as less of a hindrance, now that they had gone through a couple of interviews without embarrassing themselves. Plus, the fact that she was rough as hell was making her open up.

"I'm hoping we'll hear some new evidence today," McNicholl said once they had joined the motorway and the road was a little smoother. "The Superintendent's message said that they would be presenting the autopsy results."

"The body must have been in a right state," Rav said.

"Aye, but they'll throw all the tech they've got at it. The fact that he was in the boot of the car shows there was a criminal act, so they won't have any problem justifying the expense of all the tests. I'm hoping we'll get a cause of death at least."

"What will you tell the family?" Walker asked.

"As much as I can within my remit," McNicholl replied. "The main thing to remember is that a FL's main role is still an investigator. I can't tell them anything that might jeopardise the case, but at the same time they have a right to be kept up to date. It's a difficult balancing act, which is why this job isn't for everyone."

Walker resisted the urge to ask if she meant it wasn't for them. "And in this case, when the family has a history of criminal convictions, that must be more difficult, right?"

"Yes. We need to bear in mind that Francis Eyre is a person of interest in this case. We must be doubly careful when dealing with him."

When they arrived at Invergryff Police Station Walker led them through the building straight to the conference room where the MIT briefing was about to start. Just before they went in, Walker spotted a familiar face.

"Ah, it's yourself," Macleod said, clapping him on the back. "I thought they'd sent you off to the big school."

"I'm still at Tulliallan for another couple of months," Walker explained. "But we've been shadowing a Family Liaison officer and they were sent over to work this case. What about you, I thought you were still on medical leave."

"They've brought forward my phased return. I'm not the lead officer, but they wanted me around. Mainly because I was a spotty young constable when Gavin Eyre went missing."

"Really?"

"Aye. Only six months out of police college. Twenty years old and barely been off the islands. You can imagine it was a heady time."

"I can't picture you getting up to mischief."

Macleod smiled, a laugh breaking through his usual Highland dourness. "Don't you go fishing for gossip. Unlike poor Gavin Eyre, my past can stay in the nineties."

McNicholl and Rav came over and Walker introduced them.

"DS McNicholl has been showing us the ropes on Family Liaison work," Walker explained.

"Ah yes, you've been speaking to the mother haven't you. I

remember thinking she was a tough one back in ninety-four."

"Still is," McNicholl replied. "We haven't been getting much out of her. With the family history, they don't trust the police so she's not talking."

Macleod rubbed his chin. "Word was at the time that her man used to beat her black and blue. That was old Reggie Eyre. A right hard man. The two boys were pretty tame compared to him."

"Even Francis?"

"He got in a few fights, right enough. A couple of convictions too, for when he got a bit too rough with punters when they were kicking off in the bar. But there's plenty worse around the place than Francis Eyre."

Walker was about to ask another question when the door opened to the briefing room and they began filing in. He said hello to Neil Michelson and some others from the station and ignored the usual jokes about how he felt getting back to the front line. It was a bit strange, however, to be sitting with the detectives rather than uniform, but he couldn't help feeling a flush of excitement. He was doing it, heading for the detective ranks. Now all he needed to do was to pass the stupid exam.

Superintendent MacKinnon said a few words to explain why they were there, then he gave way to Detective Inspector Ferguson, a man Walker had never seen before. Dark-haired and slight with thin-framed glasses, he looked more like he should be working in a bank than a police station.

"I worked with him over in Leith," Rav whispered. "As clever as they come but a stickler for detail. Pulled me up on my notes once for 'inappropriate language'. That sort of thing."

Walker raised an eyebrow. A new lead officer always took a while to get used to, and Walker had been spoilt by working under Macleod for so long. He wondered what part the older DI would be playing in the investigation, but that was answered soon enough by Ferguson.

"I'm glad to say we've got DI Macleod here on secondment from Highland division where he is just returning to work after sick leave. He's done us a favour by coming onto this investigation because he was around at the time of Gavin Eyre's initial disappearance."

Macleod raised a hand to show who he was for any newcomers.

"We'll hear from DI Macleod later, but I want to start with a recap of what we've got so far. We were alerted to the presence of human remains on Tuesday morning by the council clean up team at the reservoir. You can see the pictures of the scene on the board."

On the smartboard he clicked through some pictures of a muddy area with several cars half-submerged in the dirt.

"Our remains were found in the red Escort at the bottom right of the screen. As you can see, it's a right mess, and a nightmare to process. The forensics guys have done their best, but evidence from the scene itself is largely compromised, not least due to the passage of time since the car entered the water."

Ferguson swallowed, his Adam's apple bobbing in his throat. "The pathologist is still working on the body, but as you can imagine the condition is pretty terrible. We're still waiting on the cause of death. We only got a positive ID through a DNA match. But we now know for sure it's Gavin Eyre."

Ferguson nodded at McNicholl who stood up.

"We've informed the family," McNicholl told the room. "The father is dead but the mother and brother are still alive. They are resistant to our presence. I've been allowed into the mother's house but only for brief periods. The family have a history of criminal activities and they are not welcoming any police involvement."

"Thanks for that, you might find now that we have a definite ID they open up a bit," Ferguson suggested. McNicholl sat down but Walker could tell she didn't exactly agree. Having seen both Francis and his mother's attitude to their presence, Walker was on the DS's side.

"What about the car?" Macleod asked.

Ferguson nodded. "That's going to be our best bet for evidence. It's a red Ford Escort, pretty common for the time. We've run the plates and we've had a bit of luck. Despite it being thirty years ago, there's a listing for it being reported stolen in October ninety-three."

"That's what... six months before Eyre disappeared?" Walker piped up.

"That's right. One of our actions for today is to track down the person that reported it missing, Johnnie Erroll, and find out his story."

A list of actions appeared on the screen. Many of them were related to the cars found in the reservoir.

"Once we get out of the briefing, I'm going to assign uniform to look up all these cars. I want to find out if the same person was dumping them all back in the day, or if it's just a coincidence."

Walker was glad that looking up the vehicle databases wouldn't be his job this time around. For someone who saw lists of letters and numbers dance around the page, it wasn't the best use of his mind.

"Our other line of enquiry is a list of known associates given to the police by Francis Eyre."

Half a dozen names appeared on the screen.

"Now, these are people that Francis thought his brother might have been involved with, or people that had a grudge against the family. Obviously we only have Francis's word for any of this, but I want to make sure we check them all out."

"Weren't they interviewed as part of the original investigation?" Someone asked from the back.

All eyes turned to Macleod.

"I can't be sure," the DI shrugged, "but I don't remember many interviews at the time. Remember, we had no evidence of foul play other than the fact that Gavin hadn't been in contact with anyone since he disappeared. We focussed more on his last movements."

"Could you take us through the timeline?"

"Sure," Macleod said, standing up and moving towards the board. Walker noted that he needed to haul himself up by grabbing a desk and he hoped that the Inspector hadn't returned to work too soon.

"Last confirmed sighting of Gavin Eyre was in his brother's bar, the night of the nineteenth of April. Several people at the bar confirmed he was there until eleven. His mother said she saw him arrive home that evening, but there are no independent witnesses to confirm that. The staff at the care home on Barrie Drive were expecting him in to do some handyman work the next morning, but he didn't show up. They weren't overly concerned. Apparently

"Do we have a contact for the care home?" Ferguson asked.

"The manager back then was a Mrs Marion Wright, but I've no idea if she's still with us. Must be long retired or dead by now, I'm sure she was in her fifties in ninety-four."

"We'll look her up." Ferguson gave a brisk nod. "Now you can see the difficulties we're facing. No CCTV, no social media, none of the easy investigations you young lot have been used to."

There was a ripple of laughter at this.

"But we still have our brains to fall back on. First thing is to start knocking on doors. I want all the neighbours spoken to, even those that have moved away. Track them down, find out if anyone saw anything after the evening of the nineteenth. I'll put up a list of actions and the sergeants will hand them out. I know this is an old case, but we've got a brief window where Gavin Eyre is back in the papers. Let's hope it jogs someone's memory."

The briefing broke up after that. Walker found McNicholl and Rav outside.

"Do you think they'll let us help with the investigation?" Walker asked.

McNicholl gave him a shrewd look. "You're meant to be on a placement with me, or don't you remember that?"

Walker put his hands up to acknowledge the rebuke. "Sorry. I just meant that if we weren't due to be with any family members, maybe we could help out here."

McNicholl shrugged. "Well, I have a report to write, but maybe you could ask the man yourself."

Ferguson was walking past at that moment. Rav had decided to turn his back and talk to someone else, so Walker thought it best just to take the chance while he had it.

"Can I have a quick word, sir."

DI Ferguson gave him a cool glance. "It's DS Walker, is that right?"

"Just sergeant at the moment. I'm currently going through the process of moving to SCD. Myself and Sergeant Sangar are attached to DS McNicholl."

"Ah yes, it's Ruth isn't it? You've done well just to get over the threshold with the family."

McNicholl smiled. "Thanks sir."

"We were wondering... well, I was wondering if you might need some more assistance with this case, seeing as the DS doesn't need us at the moment."

"Let's grab a word in my office," Ferguson said. Walker's heart dropped. Nothing ever good came of someone offering to speak to you in their office. As he followed Ferguson he pointedly ignored Rav miming an 'uh oh' face behind his back.

"You want to join the team, is that right?" Ferguson asked as soon as they arrived in the tiny room that was currently the office of the Senior Investigative Officer.

"Yes sir. I feel like we've already got a good grounding on the case and I would like to continue in the role."

"I'll be frank," the DI said. "I have heard that you have a reputation for being unconventional."

"Thanks," Walker replied before his brain could catch up with his mouth.

"I didn't say it was a compliment."

"Oh."

"Word is that you have some connection with a group of

private investigators. And that you've not always followed procedure when it comes to your own investigations."

"I think I have always stuck to the code," Walker replied cautiously.

The other man scratched at his neck. "It might be seen as a positive, that tendency to think outside of the box, do whatever it takes to get a result. That seemed to be the opinion of your superiors in Invergryff."

"And would that be… your opinion?"

A tiny edge of a smile appeared on the man's lips, although it might have been a smirk. "That remains to be seen. I won't tolerate recklessness here. More than in uniform, in CID you need to have each others' backs. And if you're willing to risk your colleagues…"

"I have never done anything to put another officer in danger. There are dozens of people that would back that up," Walker said, his voice rather tetchy.

"You're not in court, sergeant," the other man replied, the smile disappearing.

"Yes sir. Sorry." He took a deep breath. "The way I see this case going, sir, is that it's not your conventional murder case. So maybe you need some unconventional officers on your team. And apart from anything else, with what Rav and I have learned from working the FL role for the last couple of days, wouldn't it be a waste to send us back to Tulliallan?"

DI Ferguson checked his watch. "Fine. For as long as

McNicholl is here, you and Sergeant Sangar can work the case too. But I expect top level standards of behaviour from you both. Just because you haven't got the official title of detective yet, doesn't mean that I won't be holding you to the same standards as all the other members of SCD. Got it?"

"Yes sir," Walker said happily.

"Then take that smirk out of my office. I've got work to do."

Chapter 11: Bernie

It was weird walking back into the Corner Bells after all these years. Bernie could have sworn the same guy was dozing in a corner, an unread newspaper on the table in front of him. But then the guy from ninety-four would probably be dead by now, she reasoned. At two o'clock on a Thursday afternoon the whole place looked like it had been dug up from the nearby churchyard.

"Is Francis about?" Bernie asked the bored-looking barmaid. The young woman was in her twenties with slicked back hair and a tattoo of some manga show on her arm.

"He's just popped out to the bank."

"I'll have a gin and tonic then while I'm waiting," Bernie said. The girl handed her a glass that was more ice than tonic and Bernie perched on a bar stool. She would have brought out her laptop and got some work done, but she was sure it would stick to the countertop. It was reassuring in some ways how little the bar had changed, although she was glad to see that the smell of smoke had gone, to be replaced with stale beer and just a hint of BO.

"I hear you're looking for me?"

All of Francis's muscles had settled in a pot belly, but his arms and legs were thin. He was a shadow of his former self. He had never exactly been handsome, but now he looked like someone life had forgotten about.

"That's right. I'm a private investigator and I'm looking into your brother's death."

The pale eyes narrowed. "So why the hell would I want to speak to you?"

"Because we both know that the police aren't going to solve this one. I reckon you need all the help you can get."

That made him pause. "There's an office through the back," he said, and he led Bernie that way, ignoring the stares from the barmaid.

The décor in the office would have been dated back in the nineties. It had a brown pattered carpet and a black leather armchair that was flaking apart at the seams. The only incongruous thing was a large monitor and a fancy-looking PC on the desk.

"Make it quick," Francis said, gesturing to the only other chair in the room.

Bernie sat down, resisting the urge to hand sanitise the whole place before she did so. "I'm not here to waste your time," she promised. She still couldn't get over the change in Eyre. His grey skin and lack of teeth made him look a couple of decades older than he was. Nothing had diminished in his eyes, however, and he gave Bernie the same dismissive look he had done decades earlier.

"I'm not interested in rehashing the past," he said. "The police couldn't find out what happened to my brother back in ninety-four, so why would they be able to catch his killer now?"

"My thoughts exactly," Bernie said, nodding in agreement.

"Really?" Francis looked surprised. "You're not going to tell me this is all going to be figured out just as soon as they get the killer's DNA or whatever."

"Shouldn't think so," Bernie shrugged. "Not going to get much evidence from what's left of your brother, are they? Nah, the police are just as useless now as they were back then. We both know that."

"Right," Francis said, pulling at a hair on his chin.

"But someone like me," Bernie leaned forward, "I'm just the sort of person to solve this. For a start, I was there at the time. I know who was hanging around Invergryff thirty years ago. Half of those police officers at the station weren't even born then."

Francis nodded. "True. Spotty kids, that's what they look like these days."

There was a moment of companionship where they each considered how rubbish and disgustingly young the local police force could be.

"Anyway," Bernie said, leaving her reverie, "If you help me out I think we can solve this together."

"You don't think I'm the killer then?" Francis asked.

Bernie raised her eyebrows. "I haven't ruled it out. Let's face it, you're not scared of a little violence."

Francis grinned. "You know my reputation then. And you think I could have, what, beaten my brother to death?"

"I'm not ruling it out," Bernie replied.

The grin vanished. "So you think I might be the murderer but you still want my help."

"Why not? The way I see it, if you lie to me then you're only incriminating yourself. And if you're not the killer then the information you provide me with will help catch whoever murdered your brother. That is what you want, right?"

There was that shifty look again. "Of course." Why was he being so evasive? The fact that he was willing to help told Bernie that he probably wasn't the killer, but he was definitely holding something back.

Time to crank things up a notch. "The main reason I came here today is that I reckon you should become our client."

Now the man laughed, showing his few remaining teeth. "You want paying for this crap show?"

"Why not? You've got the money. I had my colleague check out the pub's finances, so I know you have a half-decent turnover. And as our client you'll be the first to hear what happened to your brother."

"Before the police?"

"Exactly."

She watched the man's lips working while he considered it.

"Maybe it's not a terrible idea. But you'll need to show me that you're up to the job."

Bernie snorted. "You don't seem the type to check resumes."

"You'd be surprised. Don't get me wrong, I don't want to read your CV, but I'd like to know that my money's in safe hands."

"Fair enough," Bernie said. She had to admit that Francis was surprising her once again. She needed to learn not to underestimate the man. She took a notepad out of her bag and scribbled down some names.

"There are three people you could ring. One is a local councillor who we helped out with a little problem he was having with his teenage son and a whole load of class 'C' substances. If you ask him about it he'll deny it, of course, but ask him if he was happy with 'operation gym bag clean up' and he'll tell you he was perfectly satisfied."

"You covered up a drug deal? Doesn't seem very civic minded of you."

Bernie laughed. "Not quite. The lad needed a scare so we made sure he was lifted with a half kilo of your finest icing sugar. A friend from the police station put the fear of God into him. Nothing illegal, but a minor problem dealt with."

"And what about major problems?"

"Like a murder investigation you mean?"

Francis nodded.

"Well we've solved plenty of them too. Just check the local papers."

"I believe you. You don't seem like a liar."

"My friends tell me I'm incapable of it," Bernie said. "For some reason they don't seem to think it's a good thing."

Francis tapped his foot against the leg of the chair. "Do you know, I could swear we've met before."

"We did once. I went to see you just after Gavin disappeared."

He frowned. "You must have been a kid then."

"Just turned eighteen. Oh, and about six stone heavier."

A glint of recognition flashed in his eyes. "You were the fat lass that kneed me in the balls? Christ, I should knock your teeth out. I walked funny for days after that one."

Bernie shrugged. "It was before I learned that words are more powerful than physical violence."

"Was that an apology?"

"It's as close as you're going to get." Bernie tilted her head to look at the man. "And you're still everyone's number one suspect."

"Then you're as clueless as the polis. Why would I kill my brother?"

"From what I remember, Gavin wasn't the brightest spark ever. Maybe he had become a liability in your little enterprise."

Francis hissed a breath in through his broken teeth. "You act like I was some big time gangster or something."

"Weren't you?"

"Nah. Sold a bit of blow, knocked out a few knee-caps, the usual stuff you have to do if you run a pub in the sort of area I did. But I was never in the big leagues. Never anywhere close. Certainly never anything big enough to kill my wee brother."

"All right, I'll take your word on that for the moment. Besides, I'd rather not have a murderer for a client."

"I didn't realise I'd agreed to that yet," Francis said, but she could see the hint of a smile on his lips.

"You will. Now tell me who you think killed Gavin. You've had thirty years to put a theory together. You must know something"

Francis spread his hands out on the desk. "I thought I knew at the time for sure. Francis wanted to play around with the big boys. Thought Invergryff was a bit too small or something. But as you said, he wasn't the brightest. So when he disappeared… well, I thought one of the big shots from Glasgow had got rid of the problem, you know? But when I started asking around, no one seemed to know anything."

"You'll give me the names of the people you suspected? And anyone you spoke to at the time."

"Sure. I gave them to the police and all, for all the good that did."

Bernie didn't bother repeating exactly what she thought about the chances of the police getting anywhere on this case.

"All right, send me over everything you have," she said, giving him her card with her WWC email address. "We've already got started on the case, but we'll need your help going forward."

"He was just a stupid lad," Francis said, leaning back in his chair. "That's what pissed me off about it all those years ago. He never got the chance to grow up and get any less stupid."

Bernie nodded. "I'll show myself out," she said, knowing she wouldn't get any more out of Francis today.

"Are you single?"

"Excuse me?" It wasn't often that Bernie was lost for words, but she found herself gaping at the man.

Francis grinned. "You're a fierce lassie and I like a challenge."

"No I am not," Bernie said, trying to regain her composure. "And I'll remind you that I am at work and I should not be sexually harassed."

A barking laugh filled the room. "Like when you kneed me in the balls at my work you mean?"

He was still laughing when Bernie showed herself out of the office.

Chapter 12: Liz

Everyone said that the second child was easier as you knew what you were doing. Unfortunately, with a decade between her two kids, Liz had managed to forget everything she had learned the first time around. Perhaps that was why she was finding little Isioma's toddler years a complete and utter nightmare.

"Sean, you can't leave your dirty football boots here!" she called out to her son who came stomping in from the kitchen.

"Why not? They needed to dry," her son explained, taking the offending articles away.

"Because Issy was sucking the mud off the laces."

Face wiped clean, Issy looked up and grinned with her four teeth. "No eating shoes," Liz reminded her as she toddled off to cause havoc somewhere else.

A toddler and a teenager in the house at the same time. That certainly wasn't something that Liz had planned for. Issy had been a welcome surprise after years of trying for a second child that they had thought would never come. And Liz knew she was a blessing. It was just hard to remember that some days.

"Blup," Issy said as she sicked up a mouthful of mud onto the carpet.

By the time Liz had cleaned up her daughter and the floor she had lost another hour and she still hadn't got around to the research Bernie had sent her. Of course, she wasn't meant to be even trying to work today. She and Dave had worked out a schedule so that they could both work around their childcare duties. But murders didn't happen every day, even though it felt like it, and Liz was dying to get into the Gavin Eyre case.

She could understand why Bernie was so obsessed by it. To solve something that the police hadn't got anywhere with for three decades, well, it would be quite an achievement.

Liz popped Issy into her cot, hoping that she might have even a small nap. By the time she had added a favourite toy, the soft blanket that she liked and a super annoying machine that claimed to make 'white noise' whatever that was, Issy's eyes were drooping.

She snuck out of the room, went into the kitchen and brewed a coffee while her laptop started up. It looked like Bernie had been given some new info on the case from Francis Eyre. There was a list of names of people Bernie had termed 'gangster types', so Liz got to work.

It only took fifteen minutes to find that two of the names were already deceased, one of them by the extraordinary method of a screwdriver attack. Liz was reminded that there was something to be said for a nice, comfortable, middle-class existence.

That left her with four names on the main list and another half-dozen 'associates'. She was just about to get started when there was a wail from the bedroom.

The nap had lasted precisely twenty-four minutes. Liz stretched out her back, plastered on a smile and went upstairs to get her daughter.

"Baby is crying," Sean called out from his bedroom where he was playing some sort of football computer game.

"Thanks, I realised," Liz said. Her son didn't even look around from his screen.

Liz really hoped that Sean loved his little sister. Not when she was smearing jam all over his new computer console, obviously, or when she was screaming at him to share his biscuit. But in general, there was love there. She was almost sure of it.

"Don't worry about it," Dave had said when she had voiced her worries to him. "Brothers and sisters always hate each other."

This had not been the reassurance she was looking for. Liz was an only child, so there had been no battling with siblings in her childhood. She hadn't even bothered asking her mother. Nigerian parenting was that children should do what they were told. There wasn't ever much advice for what to do when the kids themselves hadn't got the message.

Little Issy was red-faced and outraged that she had had to wait more than thirty seconds for parental attention, but as soon as Liz picked her up, she started babbling happily.

"Time for a snack?" Liz asked and this was met with a happy nod.

"Will you come down and get something to eat?" She called out to Sean, who followed her down the stairs. Food was the one thing that could entice him out of his room.

"Want to sit with us for a bit," Liz asked a minute later when Sean breezed into the living room with a sandwich in one hand. How did thirteen year olds eat so much, she wondered. If she consumed as many calories as he did she would be the size of a double decker bus.

"Do I have to watch cartoons?" Sean said with a glance at the screen where a bright blue kitten was knitting a pair of socks for some unfathomable reason.

"Um, no, but if I put anything else on she's started doing this high-pitched scream that makes my brain hurt."

Sean tickled his sister for minute, then lost interest and sat up on the sofa next to Liz. "You shouldn't let her get away with everything," he told her in a serious voice. "You need to show kids boundaries."

"Thanks for the advice," Liz said, grabbing her laptop and pulling it towards her. "Give me a sec to see if I've got any emails."

"What's this job you're working on anyway," Sean asked, pulling the neck of his t-shirt up over his chin.

"Did you hear about the body they found in the old reservoir?"

"Aye. They were talking about it in school. They said the body was all... dissolving and stuff."

"He was a real human being once," she chided, but she kept her tone light. Liz knew what boys were like with anything gruesome. "And yeah, the body probably was in a bad state. Which means that the police won't have much in the way of forensics."

"And that means you lot can swoop in and beat them to the murderer," Sean said, jiggling the sofa as he got more animated.

"I love your enthusiasm," she said, squeezing his arm. "It might be a bit trickier than that. But Bernie's got a bee in her bonnet about this one. Apparently, she was hounding the police thirty years ago that the lad had been killed and now she's been proven right."

"She has boss level energy," Sean nodded and Liz sort of understood what he meant.

"She certainly does. But it's going to be tricky. Most people can't remember what happened last week, let alone three decades ago. Just trying to piece together what happened will be hard enough."

"Could I help you with the research again?" Sean asked. "Like I did the last time?"

Liz shrugged. "You can try, but in ninety-four not everything was going online. A lot of companies were only just starting to build websites, and the dotcom bubble hadn't really got going."

Sean gave him that look that told her she was a dinosaur.

"Wait, the internet didn't even exist before then?"

"Nope."

"It was like the dark ages, right?" he said with a smile.

"Aye," she ruffled his hair. "It was all cave paintings and inventing the wheel when I was born."

"Thought so." He started leaping around the room in caveman poses, making his sister roar with laughter. Liz put the laptop to one side and enjoyed the show. Sometimes life got in the way of work, she thought, but maybe that was all right after all.

Chapter 13: Mary

Mary waved the kids off to school on Friday morning with the usual feeling of relief. They had managed to get out of the door on time after only two false starts where a coat and a bag had been left behind. Johnny had managed to leave his shoes at home, but Mary was prepared for every eventuality and had found an old pair of trainers lurking in the boot.

"They smell of fish," Johnny had complained as she laced them up for him.

"That's because we had them at the beach. You remember that time with the crab incident."

Mother and son both let out a little shudder.

"I don't want to wear the stinky shoes," he said with a pout.

"Then don't deliberately leave them behind next time," she told him. "Let me guess, you thought you'd get a day off if you had no shoes."

Johnny shrugged, then hung his head.

"Look, we'll do popcorn and a movie after school and you can pick," Mary said, trying to make sure he went into class in a better mood.

"Can we do Jaws again?"

Mary flinched. Letting the kids watch that movie hadn't been one of her best decisions. "All right, but I'm fast-forwarding through the bits where people get eaten."

Johnny pulled a face, but he skipped off into school in his stinky shoes in a much better mood.

Mary made her way back to the car and opened the glove compartment. She pulled out an emergency chocolate bar, whipped off the wrapper and started to munch. It was early to resort to chocolate, but sometimes motherhood was like that.

After a couple of bites, Mary noticed that her phone was buzzing in her pocket and she wasn't surprised to see Bernie's name come up.

"I need you to have a word with that boyfriend of yours."

Mary groaned. "What has he done this time?"

"I want him to make sure those idiots at the station are keeping a close eye on Francis Eyre. Now that he's our client I need to stop accusing him of murder quite so much. And that man talks a good game, but he's as trustworthy as... well, as a pub landlord with a criminal past."

"I'm sure they're aware of that," Mary said. "And besides, he's shadowing the Family Liaison, so it's not like Walker can tell the guys at the station what to do."

"That wouldn't stop me," Bernie replied.

"I know. Look, I've been doing some digging about something that Mrs Eyre told me."

"Oh yes?"

Mary thought over what to say. "It might be nothing, but Mrs Eyre thought that Gavin might have been seeing someone."

"Really? I didn't find any hint of that. And Francis never mentioned it."

"I know," Mary said, being careful not to sound like she was accusing her friend of missing something. "Gavin's mother said even she wasn't aware of it at the time. But looking back she reckons he was staying out at night, being secretive, spending more money than usual…"

"That could have been drugs or something else dodgy," Bernie replied. "Remember the sort of man his brother was."

"True," Mary said. She couldn't help but think that Bernie was being blinkered on this one. They didn't have any proof so far that his brother had anything to do with his disappearance. "But I want to look into the possibility that he had a girlfriend."

"All right. You could start with Jimmy Bain. He was one of Gavin's pals at the time, according to the list Francis gave me. I think he's still around Invergryff somewhere. He was a gardener or something. It'll be in my files."

"Thanks Bernie, I'll check him out."

"And you'll chase up Walker for me?"

"Of course," Mary said, crossing her fingers behind her back.

Bernie hung up the phone and Mary took a couple of deep breaths. A call with Bernadette Paterson always made her feel like she'd been in a boxing match and lost.

She took out her phone and did some internet searches for Jimmy or James Bain. Unfortunately, it was a pretty common name, so she had to wade through a lot of duds before she got a hit on a site called Platinum Landscaping. It was a basic website, just a couple of before and afters of lawns with the colour saturation up full and a phone number to call for quotes. Mary considered her own back garden which had a sad scrap of lawn that was mainly used as Invergryff's most overcrowded football pitch and the front garden which had a paddling pool that was so green with algae the kids called it a frog pond. A gardening service would take one look at her place and drive the other way. Then she thought of Liz's nice house in the suburbs with its immaculate hedges and perfectly trimmed topiary. Liz Okoro would be a much better candidate. Time to make some calls.

Fifteen minutes later, Mary arrived at Liz's with a box of toys and an apologetic smile.

"Why on earth am I to expect a visit from a gardener this morning," Liz said when she opened the door. "I was meant to be going shopping. My mother even agreed to have Issy for the afternoon."

"I'm really sorry," Mary said, understanding how precious those free hours were when you had a toddler at home. "But it's for the Gavin Eyre case. One of Gavin's best friends from school is a gardener now and I thought we could get him to open up with the promise of some work."

"And you didn't want him doing your garden?"

"I didn't think trimming two half dead rose bushes would quite get us the intel we need."

Liz sighed. "I suppose I can find something for him to do. Reckon Bernie will cover it out of expenses?"

"Probably not."

"That's what I thought. Let's have a cuppa while we wait."

Mary relaxed into her surroundings as they sat at the kitchen island while Liz brewed up the drinks with her fancy Italian coffee maker. Liz might not believe she was the posh one in the group, but her kitchen said otherwise. Yes, there was the usual child clutter, only increased by the box of toys that Mary had brought from her loft. But underneath it was a luxury kitchen, an extension that hadn't been done by someone's uncle as a favour and flooring that probably cost more than Mary's entire house.

"How is Dave getting on?"

Liz smiled. "Just the same as ever. Adding a toddler into our lives doesn't seem to have phased him at all. He's the most laid back person I've ever met."

Mary wondered if that was because Liz seemed to do all the work where the kids were concerned, but she decided it wasn't her place to say anything.

"And Sean? How's he doing?"

Now a wrinkle of concern appeared on Liz's brow. "He's good. I mean, considering what he could be like as a young teenager, he's probably pretty brilliant. But he does find Issy a challenge."

"It's hard to juggle the different ages," Mary agreed. "Do you manage some one-on-one time with the two of you?"

"Not so much. He gets plenty of boy time with his dad and his grandad, mainly when they go to the football. The only time he seems to spend with me is when we're talking about WWC business, and I'm not sure that's a habit I should get into."

"If it's something that gets you guys talking, then I'm all for it. I went through a bad spell with Peter last month when all he wanted to do was play on his computer games and ignore everyone else in the family."

"What did you do? Take away the console?"

Mary snorted a laugh. "Nah, the opposite! I bought myself a headset and now I play right along with him. It's amazing what a bonding experience it is gunning down enemy soldiers together."

Liz didn't look too convinced. At that moment the doorbell rang.

"All right, let's go see what this guy has to offer."

Jimmy Bain had the bronzed skin of a man that had spent his

life outdoors. He wore a cap to cover his bald head and he had stubble that was turning grey. By Mary's maths he was around fifty, so compared to a lot of associates of the Eyre family he seemed to have aged quite well. He wasn't dead, for starters.

"This is a nice place you've got here," he said once Liz had introduced herself. "I've done some work for Fiona Waterman up at number sixty-seven. What is it that you're needing done?"

"Oh, I thought we could start with some work on the back fence. Maybe some screening planting?" Liz said. Mary was impressed at how knowledgeable she sounded, especially as they had had to do an internet search for "common gardening terms" five minutes before Jimmy Bain had turned up.

"Right, I can see where you might want something out here," Bain said, sucking his teeth in prime tradesman fashion. "What about that lawn? I could do you a nice line in astroturf."

"I like the real grass," Liz said, her voice firm. "Better for the bees."

"Sure, sure," Jimmy Bain backtracked, "what about a lovely laurel hedge?"

Bored by the conversation, Mary tried to take a surreptitious look at the man instead. She found herself wondering if this was what Gavin Eyre might have looked like if he'd lived. They would be the same age, and Gavin had been a joiner, so he might well have ended up in a similar line of work. She felt a pang of sympathy for Mrs Eyre who never saw her son become a full-grown man.

"I think you should seriously consider a shrubbery," Mary suggested, hoping it was a real gardening thing and not just something she heard on Monty Python once.

"Are you the... partner?" Jimmy Bain said, with the worried look of a fifty year-old white man navigating uncharted waters.

"Just a friend," Mary replied, resisting the urge to make up some lie to cover for her presence. It had taken a while, but she had learned that in the detective game it was often better not to elaborate and leave yourself open to making mistakes.

Liz managed to struggle on through the rest of the garden conversation which seemed to be getting Bain more excited. Mary hoped they weren't agreeing to anything too expensive, but the man's face suggested otherwise.

"Would you like a cup of tea before you go?" Liz said when they had finally exhausted every avenue of green-fingered conversation.

"I brought Belgian buns," said Mary, who had in fact done just that.

"All right."

Mary was a bit worried that the two of them offering the man refreshments was starting to sound like the opening to a less than salubrious adult movie, but whether Bain had noticed or not, it didn't seem to put him off.

"Tea?" Liz offered when they were in the kitchen and the man had wiped his feet a million times on the mat.

"That would be great," Bain said. "Three sugars for me please."

Mary respected his sweet tooth. She liked a good couple of sugars in her tea when she was at home, but she generally drank it without at other people's houses, as she had a sense that most people regarded sugar in tea as evidence of weakness. This was born out when she noticed Liz roll her eyes behind Bain's back.

In Liz's kitchen they made some more small talk while Mary tried to think how to steer the conversation towards Gavin Eyre. In the end, Bain gave her the opening himself.

"Was it Invergryff High that you went to?" He asked Liz while he slurped his tea.

"Yes, left in 1996."

"You were a few years younger than me then," Bain said.

Mary hoped the man wasn't trying to flirt with Liz, but at least it gave her a reason to open up about their murder inquiry.

"You must have been about the same age as that poor lad they found in the reservoir," Mary pointed out, keeping her tone light.

Bain's mouth drooped down at the corners. "Aye. He was a mate of mine."

Mary put a hand to her mouth. "God, I'm sorry. It must be

awful for you, with it being all over the papers and everything."

"I'm just glad his mother has a body to bury now," Bain said, his eyes looking out of the window at the garden. "It'll give them closure, you know."

"If it were me," Liz said slowly, "I'm not sure I'd get much closure until I found out what happened to him."

"You mean find out who killed him?"

"Exactly."

Mary tried not to stare as the man took another gulp of tea.

"You know, I half wondered if he'd done himself in. Before they found the car and that."

"And why did you think that?" Liz prompted.

"Well, he'd been seeing this lass. And he'd been really happy about it. But then I saw him a couple of days before he disappeared and he had a face like thunder. Didn't want to talk about it, but I reckoned she dumped him."

"I don't suppose you'd remember her name," Mary said, her nails digging into her palms under the table. "I mean, it was so long ago you've probably forgotten, right?"

She half expected Bain to refuse to answer, or to ask her why she was so interested. But the prospect of a nice little earner from Liz must have loosened his tongue.

"It was Louise something. Louise Steele, I think. From over in Ayrshire."

"Funny that the papers never mentioned a girlfriend," Mary commented.

"Well, they'd already broken up hadn't they. She probably didn't want to get involved."

"Did you know her well?"

"Nah, only met her the once. Bumped into the two of them in Glasgow one night when he was taking her to the cinema. Pretty lass, bit older than him."

"Do you know what happened to her? After he disappeared?"

Bain shook his head. "Nah. I asked around, but no one seemed to know much about her. I figured the poor girl didn't want anything to do with it. Especially if Gavin had done himself in because of something she said."

"But he didn't, did he," Liz reminded him. "Now that the police are saying it's murder."

A frown appeared between the man's eyebrows. "True."

That seemed to be the extent of the man's thoughts on the matter. It was occurring to Mary that while Jimmy Bain might be a dab hand in the garden, he wasn't great on social engagement. He did however promise to pop by with a quote to do what he called 'outdoor renovations'.

"Sounds bloody expensive," Liz said once she had closed the door behind him. "Mind you, what he was saying about a barbecue area sounded pretty neat."

"For the two days in Invergryff that it's sunny enough to have them," Mary replied.

"Right enough. Another tea?"

"Yes please. Are you going to eat your Belgian bun?"

Mary was pleased to learn that her friend's answer was in the negative.

Chapter 14: Walker

For once, Walker was quite glad that he was only on the fringes of the investigation into the wrongful death of Gavin Eyre. It had been several days since the remains had turned up, but the investigation seemed to be going nowhere. DI Ferguson had let him get his hands on the list of known associates, but although Walker had begun his investigations with enthusiasm, it didn't take long to learn that career criminals weren't that easy to track down.

He had spent half the morning chasing up a man called Colin MacPherson. He had owned two pubs in Invergryff in ninety-four and had been listed by Francis Eyre as someone who might have a grudge against the brothers. After several hours of checking criminal records, national databases and property registers, Walker had discovered the man was now living a happy retirement in Florida. There was no way that they would get him over here for an interview without any evidence. The best bet was to try and get the local law enforcement to question him, but even that would need a definite lead to go on. He left a message for the Tampa police department to call him back, but it felt like a dead end.

"Are you ready to get out of here," McNicholl said, coming over to his desk. "You are still meant to be on my team, right?"

"Right," Walker said, jumping to his feet. He needed to keep the Family Liaison officer onside and not just because she would be writing his assessment later.

"Good." McNicholl led him out of the station to the car where Rav was already waiting, chewing on some gum and looking bored.

"I'm going back to see Mrs Eyre today," McNicholl told them. "But I reckon we should split our resources. I want one of you two to tag along with the officers attending the post mortem. That way if there's anything relevant to our role then you can pass it on directly. Decide between yourselves who is doing what."

Walker wasn't too sure if McNicholl was getting fed up of having two officers tagging along on every interview. But he was dying for a chance to get out of the office, and this seemed to be an opportunity. He just had to convince Rav to let him go.

As it turned out, Rav wasn't about to fight him for the invite.

"Would you mind if I stayed with McNicholl," the other man asked as they grabbed a quick vending machine coffee in the station before they set off.

"Nope," Walker replied. "But I thought you would fancy the mortuary."

"It's not... I'm not the biggest fan of the morgue."

Walker's eyebrows lifted. Was there a chink in perfect Rav's armour? "What do you mean?"

Rav ran a hand over his hair. "Look, the first time I went I spewed my guts out, okay? I try and avoid it if I can."

"I don't feel too clever afterwards either," Walker said, resisting the urge to put the boot in. He knew it had taken Rav a lot to admit any kind of weakness. "But I don't mind doing this one."

"Great. Maybe I'll be able to sweet-talk Mrs Eyre today."

They both laughed at that idea. Mrs Eyre didn't seem like the sort of person to be easily charmed. If she knew anything about her son's murder, she didn't seem too eager to share it. Walker knew that Mary had already managed to meet with the woman, and he had a horrible feeling that his girlfriend was going to have more success with that one than the police officers could ever hope for.

As he was without a lift, Walker went back inside to see who was heading to the post mortem. Luckily DI Macleod was hanging around at the back of the room and his eyes lit up when he saw his fellow officer.

"You can drive, then," Macleod threw him the keys. "And I can have a coffee in the passenger seat. Since I'm off the bacon rolls I need something to cheer me up."

Another trip to the vending machine later and they were on their way to the hospital.

"The missus doesn't like me driving at the moment," Macleod said, turning on the radio and then flicking it back off when he couldn't find a station that wasn't playing terrible pop music.

"I thought you were cleared to drive."

"Aye, I'm diabetic not bloody epileptic. But she's worried that

I'll have a hypo at the wheel or something. She worries about me. It doesn't help that she's so far away."

Walker nodded but kept quiet. Macleod didn't often mention his wife, or their life up in the islands. The relationship was a bit mysterious to Walker, but he didn't feel it was his place to ask about it.

"She's never thought about moving down here? I mean, seeing as you have to come down to the central belt so often, it must be difficult."

"She's got her own life," Macleod reminded him, but there was no anger at the question. "The thing is, with the hours we work she would just end up being on her own, but in a city where she didn't know anyone. That's not much fun for anyone. It always made sense for her to stay up north. Only now she spends the whole time worrying about me."

"But you've got it under control, right?"

"Oh, aye, I'm the bionic man with the pump now. But women always worry."

"Mary doesn't worry about me," Walker said.

Macleod laughed. "I bet she does."

"Well, not half as much as I worry about her. The WWC are investigating this case, by the way, so Mary's tracking down all the nasty folk from Glasgow in the nineties. All with no backup and no sense of danger."

A frown appeared on the Shetlander's face. "I should have

guessed they would be all over this one. But it's not the kind of case I would want my missus mixed up in."

"Exactly," Walker said, puffing out a sigh. At least Macleod understood what the WWC were like, having battled with them on cases before.

"But they're normally pretty good at informing the proper authorities before things get hairy," the DI reminded him. "And don't get me wrong, if Bernie Paterson had been around a couple of hundred years ago, she'd have been burned at the stake, but she is a damned good investigator."

"Oh, I'm not worried about them being good," Walker explained. "Somehow, by being sweet and likeable Mary gets more leads than half the detectives I've met. I just hate the idea of her being in any sort of trouble when I'm not around to get her out of it."

"Remind me why you haven't married the girl yet?"

Walker coloured. "What?"

Macleod laughed, and continued in that soft Shetland tone that meant he could get away with being extra cheeky. "You're clearly mad about her. And you've been seeing each other for a while, so what's holding you back."

"It's a complicated situation," Walker managed to say. "There's the kids, her ex, my job…"

Macleod opened his mouth but Walker managed to still any further conversation by pulling into the hospital carpark.

The mortuary and pathology lab were in the basement of Invergryff hospital. They parked the squad car in the staff area of the carpark, leaving a note on the window that would hopefully prevent any overenthusiastic parking attendant from fining them.

"Costs me twenty quid in parking every time I get tested," Macleod grumbled as they made their way into the hospital.

Walker was just happy that the conversation had moved on from his love life. They took the lift down to the basement and checked in at the reception to get their visitor's passes. Walker was glad to discover that they weren't doing the full postmortem. Due to the condition of the body, they had needed to do a more delicate procedure in the laboratory, and there was no need for the police investigators to witness that. Instead, they were meeting the pathologist for a debrief in her office.

He was pleased to note that the pathologist was Professor Ellie Rankin, a young rising star in the department who was not only good at her job, but adept at explaining complicated medical terms to people like him.

"Nice to see you again, sergeant," she said. Walker introduced her to Macleod.

"I'm afraid this has been a challenging specimen for us," Professor Rankin explained as she led them to her office. "The deterioration of the body has made our examinations difficult."

"Same goes for the case," Macleod said, shrugging his shoulders.

She gestured to them to sit down around the large desk. "I've set out the key areas that we focussed on during the autopsy on the table in front of you. I thought I could talk you through exactly what we found."

Walker was once again glad that he hadn't been in the room for the procedure. Even the photographs were gruesome enough. He felt a surge of injustice for Gavin Eyre. For someone to leave him in the mud like that was unconscionable.

A knock at the door announced DI Ferguson.

"Sorry I'm late," the SIO said. "I had to fight with the parking warden to get a space."

Macleod and Walker shared a look that said they were probably going to be going back to the car to find a ticket.

"Where are the pictures showing us cause of death," Ferguson asked, striding around the desk.

"Patience, Inspector," Professor Rankin said. "Let me talk you through each picture."

The Professor started with a lecture about decomposition and decay and Walker could feel Ferguson's frustration. To be fair, he felt the same, but he understood that the Professor was trying to cover her back.

"So, we have a larger margin of error," Rankin was saying. "And I want you to consider that when you are using any of this as evidence for the Procurator Fiscal. If I have to stand up in court, then I will make clear the conditions that we were working with."

"Noted," Ferguson said. "Now can we continue?"

"All right. Now, you can see when you look at the skull we've got some suggestions towards cause of death."

Ferguson leaned forward, but Rankin held up her hand.

"There is something I want to mention before we get to the skull, however. We found something unexpected."

She handed out some photographs of cleaned bones with areas circled.

"You can see here we found some interesting results when we looked at historic bone injuries. Did you know that Gavin had multiple fractures when he was a child?"

Walker looked around the room, but each person was shaking their head.

"How many fractures are we talking about?" he asked.

"Eight. Mainly to the ribs and a couple on the wrists. All healed naturally."

Walker considered what this meant. A kid with that many fractures would certainly have raised eyebrows if they turned up at a hospital.

"There was no suggestion of abuse in childhood in the initial investigation," Macleod said, "but it looks like we're going to have to do some more digging on that one. As far as I know there was no record of multiple hospital visits."

Interesting, Walker thought. Although if the abuse was

historical, it might have nothing to do with his death.

"Now I'm going to talk to you about the skull. As you can see we've cleaned it up." Rankin went over the process they used to do so. Walker felt his stomach churn, but he took a couple of deep breaths and the queasiness went away. By the time he had tuned back in, Rankin was showing them blown-up pictures of a head wound.

"You can see from the skull fracture here," Rankin pointed to an area of shattered bone, "we've got a probable cause of death."

There was a shuffling sound as they all leaned forward to get a better look. The pathologist had highlighted the areas of relevance.

"We're looking at a massive head trauma to the front temple. The other bones around it are intact, so it suggests this was not caused by the disposal of the body."

"So we're looking at what, blunt force trauma?"

"That's the most likely explanation. Now here's the most interesting thing. We did find some debris embedded in the wound. It looks like some sort of brick dust."

"He was hit on the head with a brick?"

"Could well have been. Or pushed with great force into one. It's hard to tell exactly, given the condition of the body. But I've sent the brick fragments off to the lab and I'm hoping they might find something useful for you."

"Could it have been accidental?" Macleod asked, playing devil's advocate. "What if he fell from height onto a brick path or something?"

But the pathologist was already shaking her head. "There are no other fractures on the body other than the historical ones I noted earlier. If it was a fall, then we would expect to see other signs of damage. With the usual caveats, I would say you're looking at an unnatural death, caused by persons unknown, by blunt force trauma to the skull."

Ferguson nodded, and the Doctor collected her papers, signalling that the meeting was at an end.

"See you back at the station," Ferguson said when they left the hospital. He was already on the radio arranging his next task.

Once the other man left, Macleod sat down on a bench and checked his arm.

"Is that your insulin pump?" Walker asked. "How are your levels?"

"Just fine, how's your bladder?" Macleod snapped back.

"Um…"

"Sorry," Macleod said, breathing out. "It's just everyone around me is looking like I'm an invalid and all of a sudden my body is the main topic of conversation."

"I didn't mean to be cheeky or anything," Walker said.

"I know that. But it's none of your business."

For some reason, Walker couldn't let that one go. "It was my business when you collapsed at the police station, sir."

They glowered at each other for a minute, then Macleod dropped his gaze.

"I appreciate what you did for me that day. It's just… well, how would you like it if your health was all anyone would talk about?"

"I'd be pissed off," Walker admitted. "Look, why don't we go and grab some lunch?"

"Fine," Macleod said, his face a little happier. "Better make mine a salad."

Walker made sure not to comment on that one.

Chapter 15: Bernie

If Bernie Paterson from nineteen ninety-four could see what was happening thirty years later, she would be more than a little frustrated at the pace of a real life investigation. Present-day Bernie was feeling pretty damn annoyed about it too. It was going on for a week since they had pulled poor Gavin Eyre out of the water and the WWC didn't seem to be anywhere near a result. So she had called for an emergency meeting to be held on Friday at four pm. This had not gone down too well with her colleagues.

"It's Friday afternoon!" Mary said to Bernie as she arrived. "I'm meant to be seeing my boyfriend. You know, the one who doesn't live here anymore and I barely ever see."

"That's very sad," Bernie snapped back. "Just like being unemployed will be if we can't get our heads around this case. Considering I've been on it for thirty years, it's not going to look good if we can't find out what bloody well happened. So go and make us some gins."

Still grumbling, Mary went into the kitchen to pour the drinks. They were meeting at the WWC headquarters, a small semi-detached house in Invergryff that they had inherited from an old friend. Annie had left them the house and Bernie had honoured her by putting a picture of the dear old soul up on the living room wall. It was a photograph of her giving Bernie the finger while having a drip fitted. Annie McGillivray had been a character, that was for sure.

"What the bloody hell am I doing here on a Friday when I'm meant to be watching the new *Jersey Shores* in my PJs," Liz said, banging open the front door. Bernie noticed that she hadn't come alone.

"You brought Issy?"

"Had to, didn't I? Dave has his Friday golf afternoon. Sean is at his pal's house or I would have had to bring him too."

"Ooh, gimme the baby," Mary said when she came through from the kitchen and spotted Issy.

"I saw her first," Bernie said, swooping in and popping the toddler onto her hip before Mary could get there.

Mary pouted. "Fine. I get the next set of cuddles though."

"She'll probably act like an angel now you've got her," Liz said, flopping into one of Annie's old armchairs. "She's been an absolute riot all day."

"Quite right," Bernie said, finding a can of nuts for Issy to rattle. "She's the next generation of WWC women. She needs to be fierce."

Bernie ignored the moans of the others as she set up the table with her laptop and the piles of notes she had been working on. Little Issy arranged a play area for herself on the rug and started happily ripping apart a roll of kitchen towel.

"We're treading water with this case," Bernie said, once they each had a drink in hand. "And it's getting on my tits. I want to start with a recap of what we've learned so far. Can you go over what Mrs Eyre told you, Mary?"

Mary nodded. "It wasn't exactly the easiest interview I've ever done. Not only is she deeply suspicious of authority of all kinds —"

"Probably because of her shady husband and son," Bernie interrupted.

"Exactly. She doesn't see the police and by extension a firm of private investigators as being her allies. But I did manage to get her to open up after a while. She gave me a few photos that I've added to the files. A bit weird that none of them were hanging up. In fact, her whole attitude towards her son was a bit strange."

"Strange how?" Liz asked.

"She seemed terrified," Mary said, frowning at the memory. "It was like her fear was stronger than her grief. And when I mentioned Francis that fear went up a notch."

"Really," Bernie said, "that is interesting. You think she's scared of Francis?"

"Or scared *for* him?" Mary shrugged. "I'm not sure."

"All right. Anything else?"

"One thing of note," Mary said, pulling out her phone. "Mrs Eyre suggested that Gavin might have had a girlfriend."

"Which is strange," Liz reminded them, "because it didn't come up in any of the news articles."

"But we've managed to get a name at least," Mary continued, "even though it might cost us a bit in gardening expenses."

"What?" Bernie's ears pricked up.

"We'll talk about it later," Liz said. "The point is that Gavin's pal, Jimmy Bain, told us the girl's name. Louise Steele."

"You've found her, right?"

Mary's face fell. "Sadly not. We're still looking, of course, but there's no Louise Steele on the electoral role, on the census or anywhere else around here. It might be that she's moved, or that she got married and changed her name, but so far she's proving elusive."

"I'll ask Francis about it next time I see him," Bernie said, clicking her tongue in irritation. "This is our first genuine lead and I don't want it to go dead."

"I'm on it," Mary said. "Francis is happy with us to keep working on the case, then?"

"For now. I told him that he would hear before the police did when we find out who killed his brother."

There was a moment of stunned silence.

"You can't make those sorts of promises," Mary said once she had found her voice. "If it's a murder case we need to inform the police as soon as we know anything. Christ, anything else could put us in serious trouble. Court even."

"Don't get your knickers in a twist," Bernie told her. "I'm sure we can work out a way to keep Francis sweet and do our legal duty."

Liz squirmed in her seat. "I don't know, Berns, I don't like it. And what happens if we discover that Francis was involved?"

"Then at least we know where to send the cop car," Bernie snapped back at them. Didn't they realise that she'd been on this case for three decades? This wasn't the time for any namby pamby approach to investigating.

"I'm worried about Francis taking the law into his own hands," Mary said, not letting the subject drop. "If we tell him who killed his brother do you really think he'll wait until the police go and arrest them? We could be helping another murder get committed."

"No need for hysterics," Bernie said, rolling her eyes. "Look, Francis is my problem, okay? I know how to keep him in hand." Which was true. She certainly wasn't afraid to give him another kick in the nuts if he got out of line.

Bernie spun her laptop around so that the others could see. "Okay, I've split things up so you can see what we need to do over the weekend. I assume we've all got babysitters in place?"

"Yes, Bernie," the other two said in chorus, then giggled.

She narrowed her eyes. "I don't want any excuses on this one. All right, Mary, I want you to keep on this girlfriend angle. Chase it up with Jimmy Bain and Mrs Eyre. We need to speak to this woman. Liz, how's the research going into that list of names that Francis gave us?"

"It's a tricky one. I've managed to eliminate a couple, but even the ones that are still local are retired and not that easy to track down. Plus there's no reason to think that any of them is more likely than the others. What we need is witnesses that can tell us who Gavin Eyre was hanging around with in the days before he disappeared."

"Noted," Bernie said. "I also want all the info you can find on the car," she told Liz. "Someone owned that thing."

"All right, but I might not have the time to get around to that one," Liz explained. "I've got some work to do on the inheritance case this week."

"What?" Bernie was distracted by thoughts of where the Gavin Eyre case was going.

"The one that might actually pay the bills, remember? The Hart family inheritance."

"Oh yes. Well, I suppose if you must then you can take some time for that case too."

"How generous of you," Liz replied, but Bernie chose to ignore her snippy tone.

Part of the problem was that they had too much work for three people. Ever since Bernie's niece Alice had gone off on some gap year thing to China, they had been struggling to keep up with the grunt work. Being busy meant more money, which Bernie liked, but less organisation, which she certainly did not.

"Mary, you're going to have to step up," Bernie said, not wanting to lose momentum. "I'll give you the car research too."

"There's only so many hours in the day," Mary said.

Bernie ignored her. She couldn't stand whiners.

"I'm going to speak to DI Macleod," she said, pointing to the note on the spreadsheet. "I want to find out what the police know at this point. I did ask Mary if she could use her feminine wiles to get the information out of Walker, but she declined."

Mary made a rude gesture with her right hand.

"So it's up to me," Bernie continued. "But Macleod owes me a favour."

"You think he's just going to tell you all about the investigation?"

"I might have to bargain a little. Give him the girlfriend lead. Not until after we've spoken to her ourselves, of course."

"Of course," Mary agreed. Bernie knew that despite her friend's protests, she wanted to beat the police on this case as much as anyone in the WWC. Winning was not the sort of habit you wanted to break.

"Right, we all know what we're doing then. Liz, try and wrap up this inheritance case as soon as you can so we can all focus on Gavin Eyre. Francis might not be able to pay us much, but I want this case solved. It's personal."

Bernie watched the others roll their eyes as they packed up

their things. But she didn't care. She might have barely known Gavin Eyre in ninety-four, but she still felt she owed him a debt. And now it was time for her to deliver.

Chapter 16: Liz

After the emergency WWC meeting all Liz wanted to do was to go home and veg out on the sofa, but she got a call from one of the Hart relatives she had been trying to track down, so her PJs would have to wait a little longer.

Liz dropped Isioma off with her mother and drove to Kilmarnock, which was a large town half an hour south of Invergryff. She had only been there once before, on an ill-fated date back in her student days with a man who wore trainers and no socks. It was not a happy memory.

Even with the satnav on her phone, it took her a while to locate the home of Caron Gibson. It was on one of those nineties council estates that seemed to be built in an ever increasing spiral. It seemed as though the house numbers had been flung on randomly, following no discernible order.

After a couple of false starts, she found number seventy-one off the main street and pulled up on the pavement outside. A large sign saying 'Beware of the Dog' with a picture of a ravenous Rottweiler on it, made her knock rather gingerly at the door.

"There's no dug," Caron Gibson said, showing her in. "It's to keep the neighbours away. And the Jehovah's."

Gibson was the first possible relative of Elspeth Hart that Liz had managed to find. And seeing as she lived so close, it made sense to meet in person.

"Thank you for seeing me," Liz said, taking a seat in the living room which was painted in shades of grey as was the fashion.

"I wanted to check you were a real person," the other woman replied. "When you got in touch online I thought you were one of those scammers."

"I can see why," Liz said, trying to look as un-scammy as possible. "I don't trust messages out of the blue either."

Caron Gibson nodded grimly. She was in her early sixties, trim and smartly dressed. The interior of the house, while not exactly to Liz's taste, suggested someone who didn't like much fuss and who kept things neat.

"So, as I explained in my message, I'm here about a distant relative of yours who died recently. When someone dies intestate – that just means they haven't written a will – then relatives of the deceased can claim the inheritance. Often people die with nothing to leave, of course, but there can be these unclaimed estates that turn up every so often."

"Right. And what's in it for you?"

Liz tried her most disarming smile. "We collect a fee from the estate. Which might sound like easy money, but we need to make sure we find every single eligible heir before the money is paid out. It involves quite extensive research."

She looked up to see Gibson's sharp eyes watching her. This woman was not stupid and she was following every word.

"You see, in Scotland the law is much more generous than in England," Liz continued. "The money only goes to the Crown if no relatives can be found. The line can go as far down as descendants from the deceased's great aunts and uncles."

"You're sure you're not one of these scammers? You're not trying to fleece me, are you?"

Liz tensed her shoulders, but she forced herself to carry on in an even tone. "Certainly not. In fact, you don't need to pay us any money at all. What happens is that if we discover that you are owed something, we take our cut out of that."

"Huh. And who was it you said died?"

"Elspeth Hart."

"Hart…" Gibson shook her head. "I'm sorry but I don't know the name."

Liz took out the sheet of paper with the Hart family tree. It was a sprawling, disjointed tree with lots of broken branches.

"She was married to your great uncle. The last of four marriages. She didn't change her name the last time, but her husband's name was Phillip Glass."

"Hang on, Glass? Are you sure?"

"Yes," Liz said. She had been staring at these documents for days, but she was pretty sure she had it figured out.

"His son, Bill, was an absolute arsehole. Took my mum's car and never gave it back. That whole side of the family were always on the take."

"This would be William Glass? Died ten years ago?"

"That's him. Good riddance. I went to the funeral, the whole lot of those Glass men were steaming drunk and then they started fighting over who got to keep his season ticket."

"Families can be tricky, if you just –"

"And one of the Glass lassies, Annabelle I think her name was, was wearing this low-cut black dress and started cosying up to my Tam. At the funeral!"

"A distressing time for you all," Liz said, wishing Mary was here. She was much better with irrational civilians. Liz was not quite as blessed in the patience department.

As Caron grumbled about old grudges, Liz looked out the paperwork.

"So if you're happy that you can prove this connection to the Glass family –"

"A bunch of whoring bastards, if you'll pardon the language. Never wanted anything to do with a single one of them."

Liz coughed. "There might be a substantial inheritance at stake."

"Well, blood is thicker than water, I've always said that," Mrs Gibson said without missing a beat. "And maybe we've been a bit too harsh on the lot of them."

It was all Liz could do to keep a straight face.

"We would have to prove the familial relationship, of course," she told her. "And we need to make sure we find all of your cousins and notify them. We've got to ensure we satisfy the legal requirements."

"And how would we do that?" she asked.

"Birth certificates, marriage records, that sort of thing. I've managed to access some of them already through the online Registrar General of Scotland portal, but I'll need a copy of your birth certificate and your father's one too."

"All right. I've got a load of boxes of family papers up in the loft. I suppose I could have a look through them." Mrs Gibson swallowed. "Just how substantial are we talking?"

"Well, it will have to be shared with other family members of course, and it sounds like there's a lot of them. But it should still be several thousand pounds for each of you."

Mrs Gibson's smile broadened. "I could buy a new hot tub. The neighbours burst the old one on purpose. That'd show that bitch at number seventy-four."

Liz felt it best not to ask for the details of that one.

"Great. I'll be in touch."

Chapter 17: Mary

It was nearly eleven at night on a Friday and Mary Plunkett should have been tucked up in bed binge-watching *Supernatural* like usual. Gone were the days of her teens and twenties when she would have relished the thought of being out on the town, staying up late and tottering home in bare feet because she couldn't do heels. Now she was a woman in her mid-thirties staring out of the windscreen at all the youngsters having fun.

She unpeeled the wrapper off a bar of Dairy Milk and took a bite. It wasn't a stake-out, not as such. She was just waiting for Louise Buchan, formerly known as Louise Steele, to finish her shift, which was due to end at any moment. Still, these things always went easier with a little hit of sugar.

Another couple staggered out of the bar and Mary watched them go with mounting anxiety. The photograph of Louise on her social media was clearly taken in soft focus, with plenty of make-up and a holiday tan, so Mary was concerned she might not recognise the woman at all.

She sighed and put the rest of the chocolate bar back into the glove compartment. There was nothing for it, she was going to have to venture inside. At least she was wearing her least saggy leggings and a top that had been bought in the last decade. Probably.

Luckily for Mary the bar was almost empty.

"We're closing in five minutes," a man-mountain bouncer told her when she stepped inside the door.

"I know, I'm not in for a drink. I'm looking for Louise Buchan."

"That's the manager. Should be around the bar somewhere." Job done, the huge man turned towards a man in a damp shirt who looked like he would need carried home. Mary shuddered. When you were sober the drunks always seemed so pathetic. When you were drunk yourself of course they seemed like the life and soul of the party. It was almost enough to make her swear off gin entirely.

In the end, she spotted Louise easily enough. Everyone else behind the bar was in their late teens or early twenties and the one barking orders at them could only be the manager.

"Hello," Mary said, finding a space at the bar. The floor was sticky and she just had to hope that her boots would survive the evening. They were her last remaining items of footwear that weren't novelty trainers.

"Sorry love, last orders have already been called," Louise said. She was a strong-looking woman, skinny verging on gaunt but with upper arms that either suggested a lot of visits to the gym or that lifting beer kegs might be hard work.

"I'm here to chat with you, actually. Is there somewhere we could have a quick word?"

Liz was instantly defensive. "Why? What's it about."

"Probably best if we chat in private. It's a legal matter," Mary said, not wanting to say the word murder in front of the people nearby.

"Do I look like I've got time for that? I've got to get the last of these folk out of my bar and clean up before I get to my bed. I've already worked twelve hours as it is."

Mary looked at the mop and bucket leaning against the bar. She picked up the mop and wrung it out. "Let me give you a hand then."

By the time Louise was putting the chains on the front door twenty minutes later, Mary was starting to enjoy herself. It was amazing how much more satisfying cleaning was when there wasn't a gaggle of kids around to instantly mess the place up again.

"You did a good job there," Louise said once Mary had helped her stack the glasses into the dishwasher. "But I'm dying to know what the hell you think you're doing. No one comes and works for free, do they."

Mary tried for a friendly smile. "I shouldn't think so. I didn't want to say anything in front of your staff, but I'm here about Gavin Eyre."

A glass smashed into the tiled floor.

"Crap." Louise's eyes didn't leave Mary's.

"I'll clean that up," Mary said quickly.

"No, leave it. Let's go through the back. And I'll need this and all," the woman said, grabbing one of the industrial-sized bottles of vodka on her way past.

The office was small but tidy, with lockers on one side for staff and a desk for the manager. Louise sat down behind this and Mary pulled up one of those horrible squeaky fake leather chairs that always made her thighs sweat.

"I saw on the news that they found him," Louise said, pouring herself a large vodka into a mug that was sitting on the desk. "Couldn't believe it. You're not the police though, are you?"

"No. I'm a private investigator."

"I see." Normally people asked more questions after that, but Louise just stared at her drink.

Mary bit her lip. She wasn't too sure how to ask the question she really wanted, which was why Louise had stayed out of the case, so instead she went back to basics.

"How did you guys meet?"

Louise managed a crooked smile. "In the pub. How people used to meet before dating apps or whatever it is they do now."

"Was this his brother's pub?"

"God no. Not that dump. I had some standards back then at least. We met in Glasgow, actually, in a bar on the Southside. I think it was something like the Park Inn? Long gone now of course."

"And you went out for a couple of months?"

Louise shrugged. "I'm not even sure if it was as long as that.

Six weeks maybe? I probably wouldn't even remember him now if it wasn't for what happened."

Mary leaned forward. "I would like to hear about it from your point of view. There are so few people around that remember Gavin."

"What can I say? He was just a lad. We weren't ever going to get married or anything. But he had the gift of the gab and we had a good laugh together. And I was at that age where I wanted a bit of a bad boy."

"Was he bad?"

She shrugged. "He hung around with some dodgy people. All his work was cash in hand, so he could flash it about a bit. And I liked that at the time."

She glanced up at Mary as if to check if she was being judged.

"We're all like that when we're young, right," Mary replied to soothe the woman.

"Right. So that was pretty much the extent of the relationship. I mean, it wasn't even really a relationship. We just hung out with each other for a couple of months."

"Did Gavin feel the same?" Mary asked. "I mean, did he just view it as a casual thing too."

"As far as I know. We certainly never talked about a future together or anything." She took another drink. "It would never have worked anyway. His family were a total nightmare."

"Yeah. His brother had quite the reputation."

"Francis? Aye, he was a bit of a hardcase right enough. But it was the mother that used to give me the shivers."

Mary's eyebrows creased. "Mrs Eyre? Why would that be?"

For the first time, Louise seemed unsure. "I just... well, she seemed like a tough lady, that's all. I never met her though."

"But she made an impression on you?"

"Oh aye. She didn't seem to approve of me much. And from what he said I got the feeling that she was kind of protective of Gavin."

"I see."

"Look, I've to be up early tomorrow," Louise said, getting to her feet. "There is nothing much I can tell you anyway. You're just wasting your time."

"Oh, I've nothing better to do right now," Mary replied. "Maybe I could just ask a couple more questions. Why did you break up with him? Or was it the other way around."

Louise grimaced. "I broke up with him. But it was over anyway. I reckoned he was seeing someone else."

"Really?"

"Yeah. Women always know, don't they?"

In fact, Mary had found during her time at the WWC that sadly women often did not know.

"He just didn't seem quite as interested in me," Louise continued. "Kept cancelling dates, like he had somewhere else to be. But it was some*one* else, wasn't it?"

Mary looked at her watch. It was getting beyond late. "The thing is, Louise, don't you think you should have spoken to the police? Even if you had broken up a couple of weeks beforehand then they would have wanted to speak to you."

"What was the point? Besides, I was seeing someone else by then. I know, I've always hated being single. I met this guy from the merchant navy, but he was the jealous type. The 'give you a slap if you step out of line' type. The last thing I wanted to happen was for my name to be in the papers."

That made sense, Mary thought, even if she thought it was a little cowardly. She had decided that she was going to pass on Louise's details to Walker anyway, but there was no need to tell the woman that.

"How did you track me down?" Louise asked as she pulled the chain over the door. "I didn't think anyone had connected me to Louise Steele for years."

"A lot of social media stalking. I knew your maiden name, that was given to us by one of Gavin's old pals. But I had no idea what your last name might be. So I went back to the census records. You can get them online. In nineteen ninety-nine there had been a Louise Steele living with a man named Ernie Buchan."

"Crap."

"Look, if I can find you then the police can too. Maybe you should go and talk to them."

Louise didn't reply to that one, simply opened the door of the bar so that Mary could leave. By the time she got back to her car someone had done a wee against the back wheel. Maybe she didn't miss going out on a Friday quite so much after all, Mary thought.

Chapter 18: Walker

Walker sat opposite the prettiest woman in Invergryff and tried not to mind that she was wearing a 'Dollie did it First' hoodie with Taylor Swift's face on it.

"It's so nice to get out for our date night," Mary said, smiling at him from across the table. "Especially as this is such a delicious brunch."

"I suppose. It's a bit weird that 'date night' is ten o'clock on a Saturday morning though," Walker said as he topped up his tea from the teapot.

"True, but we have to take babysitters when we can get them, and this is the only time that my mum would do this week," Mary explained. "I've already been getting a lot of mum-guilt from the kids for how much I've been working this week."

Walker sopped up his fried egg with a piece of toast. "Bernie has her hooks into this case, doesn't she?"

Mary squirmed in her seat. "Well, she's been wondering what happened to Gavin Eyre for thirty years, so you can't exactly blame her."

He wished that she wasn't always quite so defensive when he dared to criticise any aspect of the WWC. "I know that. And she's doing a pretty good job so far."

"Better than you lot," Mary said, her mouth curling into a

teasing smile. "Seems to me like Bernie is running rings around you this time."

Walker was a little stung by that. "Well, it's harder for us on this case. We rely on physical evidence to get things to court, and that's made much more difficult when it's a historic crime."

"Whereas we rely on gossip and lucky guesses."

"That wasn't quite what I meant."

He was relieved to see she was still smiling.

"Oh, I don't mind. It's true after all. We don't have a forensics lab or a pathologist or all the resources that you have. But that just means we need to use our brains a bit more."

He snorted a laugh. "And what are your brains telling you about this one?"

"You wouldn't be trying to steal my intel would you?"

Walker shrugged. "I have no problem with sleeping with the enemy."

"Oi!" Mary giggled.

"What I meant to say is: we often pool our resources. Why should this case be any different?"

"Well, for a start you think that our client is the prime suspect."

This made him pause. "What do you mean your client?"

A flush crept up Mary's cheek. "Ah, you didn't know then."

"Know what?"

"Bernie persuaded Francis Eyre to become our client for this case. Not the highest rate or anything, but enough to cover our expenses. God knows how, but she's got no shame."

Walker had to count to ten inside his head before he could reply. "So Gavin's brother is now paying you to investigate his death. Don't you think that might be a bit of a conflict of interests?"

"Only if he did it. And you have to admit it would be a weird thing to do, paying a private investigator to look into a crime when you were the one that committed it."

"People do weird things," Walker told her. "Especially criminals. Let's face it, they're often not the brightest."

"Yeah, but whoever killed Gavin Eyre got away with it for thirty years. That suggests that they're not totally incompetent, right?"

"Right," Walker said in reluctant agreement. "But I still don't like you hanging around with thugs like Francis Eyre. You will watch your back, won't you?"

Mary put her fork and knife down on her plate. "Of course. You don't need to worry about me."

But I do, Walker thought. I do all the time. When they started their relationship, Mary had been very much the junior member of the WWC, mainly doing the admin and the research side of things. Now she was interviewing hardened criminals, getting involved with gangs and murderers on a daily basis. It was impossible for him not to worry. Mary Plunkett disappearing from his life was simply not an option.

"How is the sports day prep going," he asked, changing the subject.

"The boys are excited, and Lauren doesn't give a crap, but Vikki's having a bit of a meltdown about it."

"I thought she was a fast runner," Walker replied. "She certainly was that day we lost her at the park."

Mary shuddered. "Don't remind me. Never saw a kid run after an ice-cream van for a mile before, faster than anything else on the road. She gets her stubbornness from her dad."

"Of course she does," Walker said, biting back a smile. "So why is she worried about the races?"

"Just general nerves. And she hates the idea of everyone watching her. I was just like that at school."

"Were you?"

"Yep. I was meant to be the Tin Man in the Wizard of Oz in high school once. I got so nervous before the show started that I threw up in my helmet."

"Gross."

"Yeah. Are we having dessert?" Mary asked, her eyes wandering to the pastry cabinet.

One day, Walker thought, Mary Plunkett might look at me the way she looks at a white chocolate and raspberry muffin.

"Of course. Get whatever you want," he said, even though the thought of eating another morsel made his stomach ache. The full fry-up had probably been a mistake, especially as he had to sit a fitness test at the college soon. But it made his girlfriend happy to order something sweet, and he'd found that if he refused then she would deny herself as well. It was just one of the little quirks that made her adorable. He'd just have to visit the gym when he got back to Tulliallan.

"Do you know how long you'll be in Invergryff for?" Mary asked.

"Depends on this case," Walker said, holding up a finger and wagging it at her. "So don't you go solving it too quickly now."

"No danger of that. Although I have got a few leads."

"Oh?"

Mary laughed again. "Look, I've asked her to come to you lot herself, but if you don't get a visit today, check out Louise Buchan from Ayrshire. She was Gavin's girlfriend just before he disappeared."

"Girlfriend? There was no mention of a girlfriend?"

"She broke up with him just before he went missing. But here's the thing: she ended it because she thought he was seeing someone else. Cancelling their dates, being evasive… it could have been another girl, or I was thinking –"

"That he had got into something big," Walker finished for her. "That would explain why he had less free time."

"Exactly," Mary said. "Fits with the idea that he was playing with the big guys, doesn't it? In over his head maybe."

"I've been chasing up these old-time gangsters," Walker told her. "But half of them are dead by now. If Gavin got killed by someone who is now long dead, we might never solve this one."

"Don't tell that to Bernie," Mary warned him. "What else have you been up to on the case?"

"Well, the Family Liaison stuff has stalled a bit. Mrs Eyre isn't too keen to have us in the house. So I'm trying to find other things to do so that they will keep me on the investigation. They put me on the license plates yesterday. Well, you can imagine what that looks like for me. A jumble of numbers and letters that are in random order. My worst bloody nightmare." He gave her a smile to show that it wasn't too bad, really. "I asked Rav to help with it. He's not exactly my favourite person, but he's good with a spreadsheet."

"I think that's great," Mary replied, giving his hand a squeeze. "When I first met you, you would never have done that. Nothing wrong with asking for help."

"Hmmn." Mary had always been so understanding about his reading troubles, even pushing him to get assistance at work. But Walker knew that plenty of his colleagues still saw it as a weakness. And if he was honest, so did he.

Since Mary had been so generous with her lead about the girlfriend, Walker felt he could give her a little something back.

"You talked to Mrs Eyre yourself, didn't you?"

"Yes. I got on okay until I started asking about Francis and then she clammed up. She's not an easy woman to question."

"Yeah, that's true, but I reckon we might have to have another word with her anyway. She didn't mention any problems in Gavin's childhood when you spoke to her, did she?"

"What sort of problems."

Walker paused, not sure how much he should say. "Let's just say the pathology results showed that he might have been an unusually accident prone wee boy."

Mary leaned back, considering that. "The father had a reputation as a bit of a rough character. That would be the obvious place to start looking."

"He was long dead before Gavin disappeared though, wasn't he?"

"Aye."

A few moments passed by while Mary sipped her drink. "If the beatings were bad enough to leave broken bones then Mrs Eyre must have known about it, even if she wasn't the one who hurt Gavin."

"She hates talking to the police," Walker told her. "I don't think she's going to take it well if we start throwing around accusations of child abuse."

"True. I wonder if I could get through to her. She's tough, but it's the sort of toughness that's come out of necessity."

"What do you mean?"

"That woman was absolutely terrified of something," Mary told him. "Whether it was something about Gavin's death, or Francis or... I don't know. But that's why she doesn't want to talk to anyone. She's scared."

"What could still be scaring her after thirty years?" Walker asked. "Surely the worst has already happened."

Mary picked a last crumb from her plate. "Unless we're wrong," she told him. "And for Mrs Eyre the worst is yet to come."

Chapter 19: Bernie

"I didn't realise when you said you would buy me lunch in Glasgow that we would be hunting for gangsters," Liz complained, picking at her burger and chips.

"Stop complaining, you're getting lunch on expenses, aren't you?"

"It's not exactly my idea of a refined establishment," Liz complained. The pub they were currently frequenting was of the chain bar persuasion with cheap deals and nasty pop music on the speakers.

"You should see the Corner Bells," Bernie told her. "This place is the Ritz in comparison."

"My old job took me to the Ritz once," Liz said, a wistful look in her eyes. "All expenses paid trip to London for some accounting conference."

"But what price self-worth?" Bernie asked her.

"I don't know, but it feels like it should be something more than £7.99 for a burger and a pint."

"You, Liz Okoro, are a snob."

Liz laughed. "All right, you've made your point. Why don't you tell me what we're doing here?"

"I've been working through that list that Francis gave us."

Bernie took out her phone and found her notes app. "You already know that two of them are dead. Another one, Ben Macintosh, had already moved to Spain two months before Gavin disappeared, so I've taken him off the list. The others are all still in play."

"What do we think that Gavin was up to with these big time gangsters," Liz asked. "Wasn't he a joiner in a care home? Hardly sounds like the normal career path."

"Francis said he was ambitious. And what nineteen year old doesn't want an easy way of making money? No one ever sees it going wrong until they're chucked into a reservoir."

"Fair point. And that's why you had me doing financial research first thing this morning?"

"Correct. Hang on, I think that's our guy over there." A large man in an ill-fitting suit had emerged from a back room. Fletcher Starling, who had once gone by the nickname of 'Porridge' in his gangster days, was in his mid-seventies, but he hadn't lost any of his bulk.

"Are you sure confronting this guy is a good idea," Liz whispered. "He looks like he'd floor you with a single punch."

"Not with my Muay Thai training," Bernie told her. "Besides, he's meant to be clean now. At least, he's not been arrested for anything for a while."

Ignoring Liz's protests, Bernie led her over to the man in question.

"Mr Starling? I'm Bernie Paterson. I called your secretary

earlier."

He stood up so that he towered over the two women. "And I believe you were told that I'm not available for meetings today. I'm sorry ladies," he gave them a sneering grin, "but I'm very busy."

"Too busy to speak about Gavin Eyre?"

The grin vanished. "Too busy to sit about gossiping with a pair of middle-aged Karens."

Both women bristled, more at the 'middle-aged' than the name Karen, which Bernie had never found much of an insult.

"I think you would have a much nicer day if you did find time in your busy schedule to fit us in," Liz told him.

"Aye, what she said," Bernie glared at him. "We don't want to have to get nasty."

"Nasty? I'm not sure you quite realise who you are threatening, ladies."

Bernie had had enough. "Liz, show him the tax forms."

Liz cleared her throat. "I did some digging around this morning on your limited company, Mr Starling. It seemed to me like the turnover was rather low for the number of properties that you owned. Particularly when I looked into the commercial leases."

Starling started to grow red, the colour spreading up his thick neck to his face.

"And it occurred to me that there was something not quite right when it came to what you were declaring to the HMRC. By my estimations you are underpaying your business taxes, possibly by a factor of ten. I'm sure that I've overlooked something, but perhaps you could point it out to me."

The man's jaw had dropped. "I... I..."

Bernie leaned forward. "I am bloody well sure that my friend here has overlooked f-all. And that you have been diddling the taxman out of a seven figure sum for the last three years. So how about we have a nice little chat about Gavin Eyre and HMRC never have to know, all right?"

"Who the hell did you say you were?" Starling said, his mouth finally working.

"Private investigators," Bernie said. "Working on the disappearance and murder of Gavin Eyre."

"You're not running your own crime ring?"

"No," Bernie replied, puzzled by the question.

"Thank Christ. You'd be worse than the bloody Krays. All right, then, I suppose you better come through the back."

Triumphant, Bernie followed the man past the bar and into the office area. It was full of boxes and trollies of stuff. It crossed her mind to tell Starling that someone needed to have a tidy-up, but perhaps that wouldn't have gone down too well.

There was no desk in the room that Starling called his office, just a sofa and a couple of plastic chairs. Bernie and Liz took one look at the sagging leather and opted for the chairs instead.

"If I'd have known you were such... knowledgeable people I'd have met you in the main offices over in the Merchant City."

Bernie scoffed. "Where you could have fobbed us off on some secretary or other? No thanks."

"It wouldn't have made much difference," Starling said, throwing his bulk onto the sofa which creaked dangerously underneath him. "I barely knew Gavin Eyre back then. He wasn't exactly a big player."

"But you had met him, right?"

Starling rested a hand on his expansive stomach. "Like I said, maybe a couple of times. He was just a kid really. Wanted to impress. The kind of person that thinks if they give you a firm handshake then you'll trust them forever. I've never given two craps about handshakes."

In this, Bernie agreed with the man.

"Did you hear anything about how it was he came to disappear?"

"Nah. It was a funny one. Normally when stuff like that happens, everyone knows who is to blame. That's sort of the point of sending a message, you know. But when Gavin Eyre disappeared it was just... silence. I thought maybe he'd got himself in a bit of trouble and ran off to Spain or South America or something. That happened sometimes."

"But instead he was in the reservoir."

"Yeah, like I said, it was a funny one."

"And a well-known criminal like yourself wouldn't have had anything to do with it?" Bernie said, not willing to give up her point.

"I wasn't a criminal," Starling explained. "I was just an entrepreneur who hadn't found his niche yet."

Bernie didn't feel that one deserved an answer.

"His girlfriend thought he was distracted before he died," Liz said. "One of our investigators spoke to her. She thought he might have been having an affair, but maybe it was something else. Some big business deal going down."

"I don't remember anything particular back then, but then it was a long time ago. There were deals happening all the time, none of them the sort of things you would report to HMRC. But I don't think Gavin was part of any of them."

"What was he a part of?" Bernie asked.

"Not much. He was a kid with ambition, like I said, but he didn't have much to offer. I think he got used as a runner sometimes, maybe a driver for the odd job, but never a big player. And like I said, he was too far down the food chain for me to know much about him. The details, they were handled by other people."

"Could you give us some names?" Bernie asked. "Of the people that were around back then that did interact with Gavin? It would be very helpful."

"And I want to be oh-so-helpful to the ladies with the tax details, right?" Starling flashed them his teeth. "Well, half of them are probably dead by now. There was Bill something... Bill Thorne, but he moved down to London. I reckon Cammy might have been around then. It would be just before his wife got sick. One of the really nasty cancers it was, throat or stomach or something."

"Who is Cammy?"

"I think his last name was Venny. He was kind of what Francis was trying to be. He ran jobs between the different firms when they needed to arrange something together."

"I thought it was all, like, turf wars and stuff?" Bernie said. "You're telling me that these gangs worked together?"

"Sure, when it was mutually beneficial. But because things could get a little, well, tense, they used a go-between. Some low-level scumbag that wasn't too high-up in any particular gang. I don't know how it came about but Cammy was that person in Invergryff."

"And who did Cammy work for? Exactly?"

"Not me, although like I said he did sometimes help us set things up. He was mainly working with the South Glasgow lads. I'd say Fochaber, Grant and maybe MacCulloch over in Govan."

Bernie crossed her arms. "None of this is particularly helpful, Mr Starling. You're sure you had nothing to do with Gavin Eyre's death?"

"Look, only stupid entrepreneurs actually kill people. That just brings you all sorts of attention, not to mind the pigs on your back. Sure, I've cracked a few heads together over the years, but I've never needed to off anyone. I would view it as a failure of... well, of business acumen."

Bernie found herself believing the man. But she certainly wasn't going to take him off the suspect list just yet.

It was clear that Starling had nothing more to tell them, whether through choice or through genuine ignorance. After another few questions with unsatisfying answers, Bernie and Liz took their leave, but not before telling the man they would return.

"I look forward to it," Starling said, and his smarmy smile made Bernie want to deck him one.

"Do you know what's pissing me off right now," Bernie said as they got back in the car. "How many of these gangster types are now living cushy retirements."

"Meanwhile Gavin Eyre has spent the last three decades buried in mud."

"Exactly." She put the keys in the ignition. "I reckon when we get this case all wrapped up we should give HMRC a little heads-up about Starling. Just to tell them where to look."

"For once we are in agreement," Liz said, and the two of them drove home in contented silence.

Chapter 20: Liz

Liz had not been sleeping. She definitely had not come home from the pub lunch, been dropped off by Bernie and gone for a little post-drink nap in the bedroom. So, she hadn't woken up in a panic not knowing where her toddler was.

To be fair, and just in case social services ever asked, when she had gone for her little nap Issy had been tucked up in her cot fast asleep. Dave was outside doing something manly in the garden, so if the baby had started yelling one of them would have been there in seconds.

But Isioma hadn't yelled, and Liz hadn't woken up and now she was panicking.

"Isioma? Where are you?" She called out once she realised that her daughter's cot was empty. Thankfully it was only a few seconds before a male voice answered.

"I got her," Sean called out. "She's in the living room with me."

Sean was hopping about so much that he was making Liz dizzy. The boy had never stopped moving since he was born, but he seemed extra agitated today.

"I've got something to show you."

"Okay?" Those words weren't as frightening for a mum as 'guess what I did at school today', but she was still more than a little wary when she entered the room.

At first, she thought her fears were confirmed when she saw that one wall had been covered in sheets of printer paper. Then she looked closer.

"Is this... this is the Gavin Eyre case, right?"

"You said I could look over the files," Sean said, like he wasn't sure if he was going to get told off or not. And it was true, she had let him look at the documents on her laptop, mainly because she had been too tired to think of any objections.

"I've been doing my own research for the last couple of days, finding all these cool websites about true crime in Glasgow," her son continued. "And I thought it would be useful for you to be able to see the list of all the bad dudes and what info you had on them. So I wrote them all up."

Liz couldn't believe what she was looking at. "Woah, you made a gangster wall chart!"

"I know," Sean said, bouncing from one foot to the other with pride. "Now you can see the whole thing all laid out. Might help, right?"

"Did you decorate it with ice-cream trucks?"

"Yeah. Because, you know, Glasgow gangsters and stuff. I printed them off with your printer. Issy helped colour them in."

Liz felt a catch in her throat. "That is... totally awesome. Thank you so much."

"It was easy really," Sean said, suddenly remembering that he was a cool teenager again. "I mean, I had some spare time, so… why not?"

A tiny hand tugged at her trouser leg and a voice gurgled up at her.

"Oh, and thank you too Isioma," Liz said, scooping her little one into a hug. "That is some beautiful colouring you did there."

Isioma nodded her head and then demanded to be put down so she could jump on the sofa.

"Honestly, Sean, this is brilliant. Do you want to talk me through it?"

A grin brightened his face. "Sure."

"Will we start at the top? I guess you put Francis first because he's the brother, right?"

"Right," he agreed. "And he's connected to all these other guys. Bernie wrote that he was an 'untrustworthy scumbag but not necessarily a murderer'."

"Ah, maybe I should have warned you about Bernie's language," Liz said with a grimace.

"It's nothing like as bad as what I hear in High School, Mum," Sean rolled his eyes.

"All right, what did you write down for Francis anyway."

"Well, at first I was going to write down Motive, Opportunity and Alibi for each person. I saw that on Line of Duty once. But the thing is that the murder was thirty years ago, so none of them have alibis, at least not as far as I could see."

"Good point."

"I think motive is the most important. And in that case, I think Francis is out of the running. I mean, he wouldn't kill his own brother, right?"

"Some people do," Liz told him.

"Yeah but... like, sometimes Issy annoys me, but she's still my sister, isn't she?"

Liz tried not to show how much that pleased her. "Fair enough. What about the other names on the list?"

"Well, first of all I wrote down the two dead guys. And I was going to cross them off straightaway, seeing as there dead, obviously. But then I thought: well, they weren't dead back then, right?"

"Right."

"That means the first two names after Francis are Allison and Thomlin, both dead now but alive when Gavin Eyre disappeared."

"And going to be a bloody nightmare to investigate, since they're six feet under. Who's next on the list."

"A guy called Colin MacPherson. He once took this spade and put it between some guy's legs and–"

"I think I'm going to need to ban these websites," Liz said, cutting him off. "I'm not sure they're appropriate reading."

That earned her an eye roll.

"Anyway, MacPherson went off to America and now he's a total celebrity. He's got more than a million followers on his religious channel."

"Wow. That is interesting. Not going to help with the case if he's on the other side of the world though. Who's left?"

"Some guy called Starling, but I don't know much about him."

Liz tapped his name with her nail. "I can help you out with Starling. Me and Bernie went to see him for lunch."

"Really? Cool! Did you know that he got charged with breaking someone's kneecaps in ninety-seven."

"I... did not," Liz said, glad she hadn't been aware of that before lunch. "But Starling claims that he only met Gavin a couple of times. He gave us another couple of names to look at. Hang on, let me check my notes. Ah yes. Some guy called Cammy Venny who was a go-between for some of the higher-up guys. And three more Glasgow players, Fochaber, Grant and MacCulloch. I've not had a chance to look into them yet. Think you might be able to do some more research for me?"

"Hell yeah," Sean said, punching the air. "Do you think this might earn me a bit more pocket money?"

Liz kissed the top of his head. "If you find Gavin Eyre's killer, Bernie will keep you in treats and takeaways for a month."

"Awesome!"

Chapter 21: Mary

Mary's mother Nel had once been a teacher. That meant that she had a passion for stationery and a need to organise everyone's lives. As an adult, Mary found that her mother's personality sometimes clashed with her own, particularly when it came to opinions on housekeeping or whether the kids' clothes should be ironed. But one thing she was eternally grateful for was Nel's network of teachers which meant that she could always find someone useful.

"I'm trying to find out more about someone's childhood," Mary explained while they were sitting in her mother's house, watching the children create havoc in the garden. "It's for the Gavin Eyre case."

"Oh yes, terrible business," her mother said, using the same tone she had when Lauren had trampled the peonies.

"It is, yes. But I need to understand what he was like before he died. Do you think anyone in your teacher network would remember him?"

"He went to Invergryff High, didn't he?" Nel asked, taking a sip of peppermint tea.

"Yes. From eighty-seven to ninety-two, if my maths is right. Do you reckon you know anyone who was teaching around then?"

"It's a few years before my time," Nel replied, her brow

wrinkling in concentration. "The Head would have been David Robeson, but he's long dead. Heart attack while jogging, can you imagine?"

"I can," Mary replied. "What about anyone else?"

"Rhoda might have been Deputy Head then. That's Rhoda Leonard, the one who went to teach at the Gaelic school later on. Fat ankles, poor woman."

"Think you could give her a call for me?"

"Sure."

Mary crossed her arms.

"Oh, did you mean now?"

It only took a little more prompting for Nel to get in touch with Rhoda who was now living on the island of Barra, fat ankles and all. Mary tried not to look too impatient while her mother seemed to catch up on ten years' worth of family updates.

"My daughter would like to have a wee word with you if that's okay, she's doing this little detective thing at the moment. I know, kids, eh?"

With that introduction sorted, Mary took the phone from her mother's hand.

"Thanks for speaking to me. I'm a private investigator with a firm based in Invergryff," Mary explained, trying to rebuild her credibility after the 'little detective thing' comment. "I'm looking for people that remember Gavin Eyre."

"Oh, I saw they found the poor lad's body on the news." Rhoda's voice had a Western Isles lilt to it. "It came on just after a piece on herring fishing. Gave me quite the start."

"I can imagine. Did you know him well?"

"As well as one knows any of those teenage boys that are desperate to get away from school any chance they get."

"He wasn't academic, then?"

She laughed. "No, just like his brother. I have to say that neither one of the Eyre brothers was easy to teach. Francis was bright enough, but he was too busy messing around with his friends to put any work in. Gavin struggled a bit more, I'd say. By the time he got to standard grades he was… well, not everyone is designed for that sort of study. We had to have him suspended a few times. Nothing terrible, you understand, but when he couldn't do the work he would get frustrated and distract the other kids."

"Were you shocked when he disappeared?"

"Oh, very. It was quite upsetting for all of us. He'd only left school a couple of years before, just a boy really. It was all terribly sad."

Mary knew she had to phrase her next question carefully. "There's been a suggestion that there might have been issues with abuse in the family. Physical abuse of Gavin, that is."

There was a moment of silence.

"I was never notified of anything like that."

"But you're not necessarily surprised, are you?"

Again, Rhoda took a moment before answering. "They were a hard family. Bit of a reputation, especially the dad. Of course, if we'd been told anything about it, we would have notified the authorities."

But it's easy to look the other way if no one tells you, Mary thought, making sure she kept her mouth shut.

"I met the father once. Big man, charming on the surface, but underneath... yes, I can see him using his hands on those kids. And there wasn't the same outrage about that kind of behaviour back then as there is now."

"Gavin had multiple broken bones," Mary said, her tone more severe than she had planned. "None of them treated by a professional."

"That I certainly did not know." Rhoda sighed. "Like I said, it was normally the mother we saw. She was tough herself. After the husband died... well, maybe it was a relief for her. She certainly seemed less stressed. But if we'd had any idea that Reggie Eyre was hitting the kids, then we would have acted upon it."

Mary rubbed her eyes. The woman was so defensive she wasn't proving very useful.

"I understand. And I'm sure there was nothing you could have done," Mary lied. "Did Gavin miss a lot of school?"

"You know, he wasn't too bad. The odd truancy once he got older, but he didn't skip weeks at a time or anything."

"Perhaps it was in primary school that he was injured?" Mary said, thinking aloud. "I don't think you could send him to school the day after you broke his bones."

"That sounds much more likely," Rhoda said, and the relief in her voice was clear. "If the injuries occurred before he joined our school then we wouldn't have known about it."

"Do you know anyone connected with the primary school?"

"Sorry dear, I'd have to check the records. I'm not even sure which one he went to."

Mary rested her head against the tabletop, earning a look of consternation from her mother.

"Thank you for your help," Mary said. "Will you do me a favour and ask around and see if anyone else remembers anything important about Gavin."

"Of course, dear," Rhoda said, in the tone of someone who intended no such thing.

Mary clicked off the call.

"That was a bust," Mary said to her mother. "Too busy covering her arse to tell me anything."

"That's rather unfair," Nel said primly. "I'm sure if she knew anything, Rhoda would have told you. She was a member of the Rotary Club."

Mary resisted the urge to ask what the hell that had to do with anything. Sometimes it felt like not only was her mother from another era, but she was from another galaxy.

Chapter 22: Walker

It might have been a Sunday morning, but there were still plenty of officers milling around Invergryff police station. Investigations often had a kind of momentum to them, and Walker knew that every person in the office could tell that the Gavin Eyre case was beginning to stall.

"I don't think we'll be here come Monday," McNicholl said as she ate a supermarket sandwich at her desk. "I can't see Ferguson justifying a full time Liaison officer if there's no new leads."

Walker's shoulders hunched. He hated the idea of leaving the investigation before it had come to a conclusion. It might seem like a cold case to everyone else, but there was something about Gavin Eyre's murder that made it feel like it had happened yesterday. Maybe it was the image of the young man playing football, living his best life just before it was snatched away from him. Or maybe it was because Walker felt he still had something more to contribute, even if he wasn't entirely sure what that was yet.

As if he knew they were talking about him, DI Ferguson entered the office. His eyes looked tired, but his suit and appearance were as neat as ever. To Walker's surprise he made a beeline over to his desk.

"Didn't realise you were scheduled to work today?" Ferguson said.

"No sir. I wanted to get ahead on the case."

"You're still working through those license plates? I would have thought you'd have finished by now."

Walker felt heat rise from his neck. "I asked Sergeant Sangar to help with that, I think he's nearly finished. He's got a good eye for detail."

"And you don't?" Ferguson blinked and Walker felt like the man could read his mind.

"I'm better at big picture stuff."

Ferguson was about to reply when a uniformed officer came over to the desk.

"There's a call for you from America," the constable said. "I've put it through on line one, but I wanted to give you a heads-up. Says he's a Sheriff."

Saved by the phone, Walker picked up the handset while Ferguson wandered away to speak to someone else. He couldn't think who it could be until the man on the phone introduced himself as Sheriff Fulson from Tampa calling about a name on their list.

"You've been trying to get hold of someone who knows Colin MacPherson, is that right?"

The man's accent sounded like something out of a cowboy movie. Walker's inner child was delighted. "That's right. He's come up as a person of interest from a case here."

"Must be from a long time ago?"

"Thirty years."

"That explains it," Fulson said cheerily. "He's been over here long enough to go native. A real local character, that's MacPherson. Can I ask what the crime is?"

"We've discovered human remains, looking like an unlawful death and MacPherson is on our list of people to talk to."

Fulson whistled. "Sounds fun," he drawled. "Well, you'll be glad to know that I've set up a call with the man himself. He's agreed to chat to you, informal like."

"Really?"

The man on the other end laughed. "I know, not what you were expecting, right? But you've gotta understand that this guy is now a pillar of the community. He's even got his own TV station. A born-again Christian, that type of thing. And his whole schtick is how he turned away from a life of crime. I reckon he doesn't want anyone suggesting that he might have been involved in a nasty little murder."

"That makes sense," Walker said. "What's your take on the guy?"

"Oh, he's your classic conman," the Sheriff said with another chuckle. "Don't get me wrong, all that Jesus loving stuff doesn't fool me. He's just found an easier way of making money these days. Whether or not he was involved in your case, I have no idea. But I get the feeling that if he felt he was in trouble he would have shut you down with lawyers rather than talking to you himself."

"Okay," Walker said. "Any other tips for when I talk to him?"

"Don't send him any money," Sheriff Dan said and he ended the call still laughing.

It only took another hour until Walker was talking to the man who now referred to himself as Pastor MacPherson.

"Ah, it's good to hear a Scottish accent," MacPherson said. Walker noted that the man's own accent had more Florida in it than Invergryff. "I've been away for far too long."

"You don't make many visits home then?" Walker asked.

"Tampa is my home now. And the people here have welcomed me with open arms, God bless them all."

Walker felt like he could imagine the tanned face and shining white teeth just from the tone of the other man's voice.

"I wanted to talk to you about a disappearance that occurred in nineteen ninety-four."

"Ah yes, young Gavin Eyre. Do you know, until the Sheriff called I didn't even know that they had found his body. Poor lad."

There didn't seem to be much genuine emotion there, but then why would there be after so long?

"Did you know him well?"

"No. I barely knew him. I think I only met him once."

Walker waited.

"As you might know, I had a bit of a wild youth," MacPherson said with a laugh. "By the time that lad disappeared, I was already looking for a way out of Scotland. I'd been involved with some... let's say unfriendly characters back in Glasgow. And they were expanding into Invergryff."

"You're talking about drugs?"

Another laugh. "I couldn't possibly say that to a policeman, could I? Let's just say I was part of a firm of enterprising individuals. We were the whole package, controlling entire areas through the pubs, the local enforcer types, and yes, some less than savoury practices."

Walker was getting annoyed by all the euphemisms, but he knew that the man could end the call whenever he liked so he kept his tongue.

"Where did Gavin Eyre fit into all this?"

"He didn't, not for my organisation, but he did a bit of running for some of the others. Always on the fringes, nothing major. I don't think he was clever enough to get very far in that world. Too prone to opening his mouth, for one thing."

"Why would you say that?"

"There was a rumour, a few months before he disappeared that he might have been helping his brother out by sharing intel from some of the bigger firms. But then he was still employed after that, so it can't have been anything too serious."

"It would be very helpful if you could tell us who exactly was employing him at the time," Walker said.

"Bobby MacCulloch, big name on the South side of Glasgow. Think he got into nightclubs later on. Might be dead by now though. Many of those men who had not been lucky enough to find the good Lord like I did died early."

"Did Gavin's disappearance come as a surprise?" Walker said, determined to keep the conversation on topic.

MacPherson seemed to think about that for a moment. "I'd say so, yeah."

"And there weren't any rumours at the time who might have been responsible."

"None. Which was strange in itself when you think about it. Francis had gone around all the 'names' right after Gavin went missing. Asking everyone if they knew who did it."

"There was no doubt that he had been killed, then?"

"Francis didn't seem to think so. And I think there was some story about how he was about to come into a bit of money, so there was no reason for him to leave."

"What money was this?"

"No idea."

Walker pushed back against his desk in frustration. "But someone must have told you about it, right?"

"Could have been Cammy I suppose. He always knew

everything that was going on back then."

"Cammy who?"

"Cameron Venny. A weasel of a man. We used to use him as a sort of go-between for the street crews and the people further up. Think he was from Coatbridge or somewhere, outskirts of Glasgow anyway. We're all God's children, of course, but the good Lord certainly forgot to hand out any charm to Cammy."

"Is he still alive?"

"Might be. He had that sort of wiry physique, never saw him eat but he was fit enough."

Walker talked to the man for a few more minutes, but it was clear that the Pastor wasn't going to give him anything else useful.

"I hope you find justice for the poor soul," MacPherson said when they got to the end of the call. "At least he can rest in peace now."

The Pastor hung up and Walker stared at his notes. A couple more names from the ninety's criminal scene, but no concrete leads. If Pastor MacPherson was personally involved in Gavin Eyre's death and disappearance, then he didn't give any hint of guilt. Although if he was the con man that the Sheriff claimed then lying about it probably wouldn't cause him a problem.

Still, it was better than nothing and at least it might convince Ferguson that he was an asset to the team, rather than just a wannabe detective with an attitude.

Chapter 23: Bernie

Bernie was a little offended when DI Macleod squealed as she popped her head around the corner of the café.

"What the bloody hell are you doing here," the Inspector said, wiping the tea that he had spilled down his front.

"I've come for a chat," she said. "Mind if I sit down?"

"Does it matter if I say yes?"

"Not really," Bernie said happily. She always liked starting an interview where the subject was on the back foot.

"How did you know I was here?"

"Invergryff always put up their visiting officers in the same hotel, that rather soulless place with the garish pink doors. On the streets around it there are only two cafés, one greasy spoon and this newer place that does fancy smoothies. I figured that given your recent health scare you might have gone for the posher café."

"Well done," Macleod said, although he still wasn't smiling. "And I suppose you want to have a go at me for eating breakfast too? Maybe count the calories for me? Force me to drink one of those vile green smoothies that cost eight quid each?"

"Not really," Bernie said, shaking her head. "You've got poached eggs on toast there, so at least it's not fried.

Wholemeal bread is good, although you should probably just have had one slice. And as for the smoothies, they've got more sugar in them than a Mars bar."

"Is that right?"

"Yep. I'd say you're doing not too bad." Bernie gave him a stern look. "Gave you a hell of scare that hypo of yours, didn't it?"

For a moment, Bernie thought he would argue the point. Then Macleod gave her a wry smile.

"You were a nurse in a care home, weren't you?"

Bernie nodded.

"So you've seen plenty of folk carted off in ambulances."

Another nod.

"In my line of work I'd seen a fair few too. But I'd never been in the back of one, unconscious on a stretcher. Kind of puts things into perspective, right?"

"Right. But it doesn't have to ruin the rest of your life. And the key is that there will be a rest of your life. And you know how to make that happen."

Macleod grinned. "That was almost nice, Bernie."

"I know. Don't tell anyone. Let me order a coffee and we can get back to this Gavin Eyre business."

By the time Bernie's Americano had turned up, she had

explained her involvement with Eyre's disappearance all those years ago.

"As you can imagine, I've always wondered what happened to Gavin. And now with him turning up all these years later when I've set up my own investigation company, you can imagine that it feels like I'm meant to solve it."

Macleod wiped at his face with a napkin. "He's been at the back of my mind for all these years too. I was one of the original officers on the case. That's the only reason why they agreed to me coming back to work so soon."

Bernie was surprised that Macleod had worked the original case. "You lot made a right mess of it the first time around," she reminded him.

"I don't think that's fair. The lad vanished off the face of the earth. Plus, there was the fact that none of the friends or family wanted to talk to us, given they were none of them were exactly model citizens. No physical evidence and no witnesses either. What exactly were we meant to do?"

"Work harder," Bernie said, taking a gulp of coffee. "I would have thought that much was obvious."

"Was there something in particular you wanted to chat about?"

Bernie shrugged. "A few things, but now that I know you worked the original case, I'd like to hear what your impressions were of the family."

Macleod blew out a sigh. "There was only the two of them. Mrs Eyre and the brother. The dad had been dead for a while, five years or so. Apparently he was a nasty piece of work, but like I said I never got the chance to meet him. But that's where the sons got into the dodgy stuff, through the people their father had hung around with."

"The family business."

"Exactly. A very low-rent version of the mafia. Francis was always on our radar, but he never managed to get into the big time. And Gavin seemed to be going the same way. A bit of vandalism and stuff when he was a young teen, nothing more than that."

"Not the sort you would expect to get killed."

"On the contrary," Macleod said, "guys like him get killed all the time. Stupid enough to get involved in things above their head, but not clever enough to be useful to someone so that they let them live. The weird thing was the disappearance. Normally it would be a stabbing in the street, a body left in an alleyway, that sort of thing."

"But a disappearance is more personal, is that what you're saying?"

"I guess so. It makes me wonder if we might be looking in the wrong direction with all this gang stuff."

Bernie considered his point and found that it had some merit.

"I don't suppose you'd like to leave me alone now," Macleod said, checking his watch. "I'm meant to be phoning my wife soon. I'd rather she didn't call when I was in the middle of a meeting with a strange woman."

"I could have a chat with your wife if you like," Bernie offered. "Show her there's nothing to worry about."

"Don't you dare," Macleod said, glaring at her from under his eyebrows.

"Pity. I'm sure we'd have a lot to chat about"

That earned her another scowl, so Bernie decided to draw the meeting to a close. Mind you, Macleod had given her something to think about. If the police had been blinded by the gangster angle, didn't that mean the WWC had too? That was something that would have to change.

Chapter 24: Liz

Bernie had turned up at Liz's door in a determined mood.

"I reckon we've been neglecting some of our resources," she had told Liz while bundling her out of her house and into the car. "We're off to speak to one of my former colleagues. I just hope she'll let us in the door."

With that cryptic message relayed, Bernie drove them down to the South East of the town where they pulled into a street of small retirement bungalows.

"Who are we here to see?" Liz asked as they climbed out of the car.

"Marion Wright, former manager of the care home where Gavin worked. While we've been chasing after gangsters I've been neglecting the witnesses that were around at the time. I don't intend to do it again."

They walked up the drive and Bernie rattled the letterbox until a small figure opened the door.

"What is… Paterson!" The door would have slammed shut, had Bernie's trainer not been wedged in the way.

"Get the hell out of here." The woman was clearly furious. She looked to be in her eighties, but her anger was giving her the strength to pin Bernie's foot easily.

"What's going on?" Liz asked, looking from one face to the

other.

"Marion and I have a bit of a history," Bernie said.

"She got me fired!"

Liz joined the woman in glaring at Bernie. A heads-up from her friend would have been nice.

"It was a long time ago," Bernie said. "I'm surprised you're not over it yet."

"You've got five seconds to explain why you're here before I call the police for harassment," Marion told her.

"You saw that they found Gavin Eyre's body."

This made the woman pause. "I did, aye. Poor kid."

"That's all I want to talk about. I'm sure you've heard through the grapevine that I'm a private detective now. Any history between you and me has nothing to do with this."

"But I don't have to speak to you, right? It's not like you're the police or anything."

"No," Liz chimed in, "but I'm guessing you know what a nightmare Bernie can be if she doesn't get her own way. If you don't want her ringing your bell every five minutes, I'd just let us in. If you tell us what we need to know you'll never have to see Bernie's face again."

Marion whistled out a sigh. "Fine. But I'm not making you a cup of tea."

Bernie practically skipped over the threshold. Liz followed her, resisting the urge to give her partner a sharp elbow between the shoulder blades.

"Nice place you have here," Bernie said, sitting herself down on the sofa.

"Would be a hell of a lot nicer if I hadn't had to take my pension early," Marion snapped.

Liz was dying to ask why she'd got the sack, but she thought it best to try and keep everyone focussed on the case.

"Bernie said you were the manager of the home when Gavin Eyre was working there."

"That's right. It was me that gave him the job. I suppose I felt sorry for the lad. He turned up at the home one day looking for work. As it happened, we'd just had someone let us down for some gardening work. He cut the grass for us, tidied up the paths, and he did a fair enough job. Besides, he was cheap and as Bernie will tell you, there's never enough money in these places, especially considering the paltry council subsidies. They weren't any better back in the nineties, let me tell you that for nothing."

Marion pulled her cardigan closer and continued. "Anyway, he left his name and number and he also let us know that he had done a couple of years of a joinery apprenticeship. I don't think he ever finished, but it meant he had enough skill to do the sort of jobs we needed, building beds, repairing other bits of furniture that got damaged, those sorts of things."

"And you weren't worried that he had a bit of a dodgy background."

Marion's eyes narrowed. "I was never one for judging others, unlike your pal there."

"She means me," Bernie said happily. Liz suspected her friend was enjoying herself. There was nothing Bernie liked more than when someone was really angry at her.

"So Gavin was working for you regularly by the time he disappeared," Liz prompted.

"I wouldn't say regularly. It wasn't like he was in there Monday to Friday or anything. It was more casual than that. It would probably be once or twice a week that I asked him to come along and do some work for us. He was glad of the cash and I was happy to have someone reasonably reliable to work with. But like a lot of men he couldn't help taking advantage in the end."

"Oh?" Bernie leaned forward. "How so?"

"I never wanted to tell anyone at the time," Marion said. "I mean, his poor mother had been through enough. But I'd had to give him a big telling off just a couple of days before he disappeared."

"Why was that?"

"One of the cleaners caught him making use of one of the empty rooms for a, well, a liaison with someone of the female persuasion. The cleaner never saw who the girl was, but she heard them clearly enough. I confronted Gavin about it, and he said it wouldn't happen again. But I'd already decided we wouldn't use him anymore before he went missing. I can't have people like that on my staff."

Bernie and Liz looked at one another. Who had Gavin been sleeping with? And was it relevant to his death?

"That's all I know," Marion said, getting to her feet. "And I'd appreciate you getting the hell out of my home."

The elderly woman practically shoved them out the door.

"What the hell did you do to her?" Liz asked as they made their way back down the drive.

"She did it all to herself, I just caught her in the act. She was nicking the odd tenner out of people's purses. Only after they passed away, mind you, so no one would ever have noticed."

"But you did."

"Of course I did," Bernie said with a shrug. "And I reported it to the bosses. Rather than get the cops in, they quietly retired her. Better than she deserved if you ask me."

"She still thinks you were in the wrong," Liz said.

"People like that never admit they might have made a mistake. She kept saying: what did it matter if they had already died? A victimless crime, you might say. That's certainly how Marion saw it. But to me, a person that steals from the dead isn't the sort of person you want in charge of the living."

"Remind me never to nick anything from petty cash," Liz said.

"There wouldn't be any point. Mary always spends it on biscuits anyway."

They got into the car.

"The girlfriend never mentioned that Gavin took her to the care home," Liz said while Bernie drove. "I think Mary would have told us if she had.

"Maybe it wasn't the girlfriend. Didn't Louise say that she thought he was seeing someone else?"

"Oh yeah, I'd forgotten that. So maybe he had some other girl on the go and if he was seeing her in secret then the care home would be a good place to do that."

"Maybe she was married," Bernie said, thinking out loud. "There had to have been some reason why they were sneaking about so much. I can't think that people would choose a care home for their private moments unless they didn't have another choice."

"True," Liz replied.

"You would have to be desperate, in fact," Bernie added. "I've seen the state of the mattresses."

Chapter 25: Mary

It was Sunday afternoon and Mary's ex-husband was taking the kids to the funfair. Matt and his partner Stephanie had arrived just after lunch to collect the four children, and Mary had waved them off with a sense of unbridled joy. Firstly, because she knew that taking the kids to the fair would be an absolute nightmare of stickiness, skinned knees and whining and now she didn't have to do it herself. And secondly, because she needed to get some work done and that was infinitely easier without any children around.

There was the endless mountain of washing, which was beginning to develop its own ecosystem, that still needed to be done, but Mary knew it was more important to start work first. After all, her job with the WWC paid the mortgage, and pulling tissues out of trouser pockets did not.

She had just settled down with a cup of tea, a chocolate biscuit and the Gavin Eyre file open on her laptop when her mother rang.

"Did you see that they've shut Gentleman's Brae?" Her mother told her without bothering to say hello.

"Where's that?" Mary asked, trying to balance her biscuit on the edge of her tea.

"Near the new hospital. Traffic is backed up right to the motorway."

"Oh dear. Are you driving just now?"

"No," her mother sounded surprised by the question. "I'm doing the gardening. The fuschia has become quite out of control this year."

Mary tapped at the spreadsheet, trying to ignore the image of unruly fuschias.

"If you're at home, why are you worried about the traffic?" she asked her mother.

"I just thought I better warn you. Someone put a post about it on the local social media group."

"Makes a change from complaining about the bins," Mary told her. "Look Mum, it's lovely to hear from you but I am trying to get some work done."

"But that's what I'm phoning about."

"It is?" Half of the chocolate biscuit fell into her tea with a plop.

"Didn't I say? I was thinking about that phone call yesterday when you were over with the children," Nel said.

Mary sighed. Sometimes her mother could be frustratingly vague. "Which one? The one where we had to call the poisons line to find out about those berries that Johnny ate or the one where we had to call Peter's friend to tell them that they wouldn't be having a BB gun fight like he had told him."

"Neither. I was talking about your little chat with Rhoda."

"Oh, that one."

"Who you were rather rude about, by the way. But it got me thinking about someone that might have known the Eyre family back then."

"Yes?" Mary shoved the rest of the biscuit into her mouth before it was lost as well.

"I remembered about this friend of mine, Siobhan. Have I told you about her?"

A memory popped into Mary's head. "Is that the one that married the guy she met on a cockerpoo lovers website?"

"No, that's Siobhan Nivan. Oh, and it didn't work out with the cockerpoo guy, she's seeing a lovely man from Dunoon with a chihuahua now. This is Siobhan Beale I'm talking about."

"Who is?"

"I know her from the line dancing class at the club on a Tuesday. She's a social worker. Covered the east side of Invergryff in the nineties. So I thought the family might be known to her."

This made Mary sit up in her chair. "Really? And you got in touch with her?"

"I did," Nel chuckled. "I felt like quite the little investigator myself. I phoned her up and I said: Siobhan, I'm going to ask you some questions, but you don't have to reply without a lawyer."

"We don't normally say that bit," Mary told her, massaging her temple.

"Oh, that is a shame. Anyway, Siobhan agreed to have a little chat if I showed her how to do the Electric Slide. And I asked her about the Eyre family."

"What did she say?"

"She knew them all right. I think the school had called in social work more than once. Anyway, I told her to pop over to your place this afternoon. She was in town anyway getting her nails done."

"You invited a social worker over to my house?" Mary looked at the fridge where Peter had pinned up a picture of Stalin from their history project and the kitchen counter where Johnny had submerged two of his sister's dolls in custard.

"Is that a problem?"

"No, no… what time did you say she was coming?" Mary skipped through to the living room, furiously tidying up as she went. There was a bra hanging on the radiator to dry and she whipped it off, knowing she couldn't blame the kids for that one.

"Should be with you in a jiffy," Nel replied.

"Of course she bloody will," Mary hissed, shoving the washing pile behind a cupboard door.

"What was that dear?"

"Thanks for arranging it," Mary trilled, "I'll speak to you soon."

In fact, it was ten minutes before the social worker arrived, giving Mary just enough time to make the house look like a reasonably responsible parent lived there. She hoped.

"Please come in," Mary said when she opened the door. "Would you like a tea?"

"Yes please." Siobhan Beale was in her sixties, with grey hair shaved at the sides and a tie-dyed dress.

"Take a seat and I'll pop the kettle on," Mary told her, aware that her voice was higher than usual. There was no need to be nervous, of course. Siobhan wasn't there to judge Mary's family. At least, she hoped so.

Siobhan didn't seem to disapprove when Mary handed her a cup of tea and a plate of chocolate digestives.

"Thank you. I hope you don't mind me dropping in like this. Your mother said that you would be available this afternoon."

"Yes, the kids are away with their dad so it's a little quieter than usual." Mary swallowed and reminded herself that she was meant to be in charge of the interview. "Nel told you that my agency is looking into Gavin Eyre's death, did she?"

"You're a private investigator," Siobhan said, as if she couldn't quite believe that was a real job.

"Yes. We take on all sorts of cases, but this one is rather unusual. One of our members knew Gavin before he disappeared, so that's how it came on our radar."

"How interesting. Did she know him well?"

"Not at all. She worked at the care home. But it seems like the disappearance made an impression on her at the time."

Siobhan nodded. "It was a big story. Because he had played for Invergryff Town and he just seemed to have vanished, it was in all the papers. Our answer to the Marie Celeste, I suppose. It was so sad to read that he'd been dead all along."

"Mum told me that you knew the family," Mary said.

"Yes. Well, I knew most of the families in the area in those days."

"Why was it that the Eyre's came to the attention of social work?"

Siobhan pursed her lips. "I'm not sure how much I can say."

"Very sensible," Mary told her. "And I admire your commitment to your job. But client confidentiality wouldn't normally extend after his death, would it?"

"I'm not sure."

Mary hated conflict but she channelled her inner Bernie and gave the woman a dazzling grin. "I'm sure you wouldn't have come all the way over here if you hadn't had something to say. You can be assured that anything you tell me is completely confidential."

Siobhan picked up a chocolate digestive and dunked it in her tea. "I suppose you always wonder if you could have done more. For the kids that make the headlines for all the wrong reasons, I mean. They still with you, those kids."

"What is it about Gavin that you remember?"

"A kind of cocky young lad. He must have been around thirteen when I first met him. Then I met him again when his dad died a year later. We made a visit for bereavement support, not that the family were very interested in that."

"Could you tell me about the father, Reggie Eyre?"

"I think he was a drinker. Well, most men of that type were back in those days. Drank, smoked, behaved badly…"

"We think he was beating Gavin," Mary said. "When they did the autopsy they discovered he'd had several fractures that had been allowed to heal without medical intervention."

"Well, crap." Siobhan's face dropped. "I didn't see any of that. And if the wife won't come forward and the kids don't tell anyone then it's very difficult for us to do anything."

"I know. And I'm not placing any blame," Mary said, remembering how Rhoda Leonard had closed up at the mere suggestion that they might have been responsible for any of Gavin's childhood. "I'd just like to understand exactly what happened to him."

"Then you need to get the mother to talk to you," Siobhan told her. "And even then, I'd have told you that you wouldn't get a thing out of her. Only the husband died. That might make her more likely to talk."

"What was Gavin like after his father died? Upset?"

"Not very," Siobhan gave her a tight smile. "Although you might just have explained why. The mother seemed upset though. I remember thinking she was wound so tightly she might snap one day. But they must have done all right after that because I was never sent there again."

"I know that the boys were skipping school. You didn't go and speak to them for that?"

"Took more than missing a few lessons to get a social work visit back in the nineties," Siobhan told her.

They chatted for a little longer, and then Siobhan finished her biscuit and left. Mary stood at the door for a few moments after the woman had driven away. Something about the conversation had dredged up a memory. Was it from an interview? A wary expression?

Suddenly she remembered. It was Louise Buchan's face when she talked about Gavin's family. Moving quickly before the insight faded, Mary picked up her phone and dialled the number that the woman had reluctantly given her.

"I went to speak to the police," Louise said as soon as she picked up the phone. "So you don't have to nag me about it. That's two hours of my life I'll never get back, by the way."

"That wasn't why I called," Mary told her.

"It wasn't?"

"No. I wanted to know why you thought that Gavin's mother

was someone to be scared of."

"What do you mean?" Louise said, but she was talking a little too quickly and Mary knew that she had hit the nail on the head.

"We were talking about Gavin's family and you said you were more scared of the mother. I was just wondering why that was, given that you never met her."

"I don't remember saying that."

"Well you did," Mary told her. "And look, I'm sure you would rather speak to me about it than the guys over at Invergryff Police Station."

"Fine. It was something Gavin said once. He was pissed, so he probably didn't even mean it."

"What exactly did he say?"

"He kind of hinted that… that his mother had killed his dad."

Mary exhaled slowly. "That's what he said."

"Look, that's what I remember, but like I said it was thirty years ago. I could be wrong."

"The sad thing is I don't think you are. Thanks for your help, Louise."

She put down the phone and punched the air.

"Yes!"

It was so satisfying to find a hunch confirmed. But as she stood in the silent hallway, it didn't take long for Mary's mood to drop back down. Now that she knew exactly what had happened in the Eyre household, just what in the hell was she going to do about it?

Chapter 26: Walker

It was twenty-three degrees in Invergryff, but when you were standing outside with no shade in a plain clothed officer's cheap suit, it felt like the surface of the sun. But Walker didn't mind too much. Since he had been the one to find out the name Cameron Venny from his phone call to Florida, he had managed to persuade Ferguson to let him interview the man. It hadn't taken long to track the man down. Venny was still on the police radar. Unlike some of the other names from their list of Gavin Eyre's associates, Venny had never quite managed to go clean. The last five years he had managed to avoid jail, but only narrowly. One of the conditions of his recent release was that he had to work in the community. This was why Walker found himself watching a lawn bowls match between Invergryff Seniors and Glasgow West Second Team.

The world of bowls was not one that Walker knew anything about, but what had initially seemed to be a relaxing sport for the older population had turned into something else the longer he watched. There seemed to be a real grudge match going on, and one player had already been sent off for some unsavoury gestures to some of the wives.

He'd been standing waiting for about half an hour when he saw an unwelcome face coming out of the clubhouse.

"What's up copper," Bernie said, handing him an ice-cream. "Saw you standing out here and thought you might need to cool down."

"You better not have been following me," Walker told her, only just managing to keep from yelling.

"Of course not. You lot are so jumpy. I'm here to interview Cameron Venny in connection with the Gavin Eyre case, just the same as you must be. Or have you decided to start a new hobby?"

Why did she always manage to get under his skin? He felt like throwing the ice-cream back in her face, but then it was getting rather hot.

"I hope this isn't an official bribe," Walker said, taking a lick.

"Not at all. I'm guessing you worked out where Cammy has been doing his community service too."

He nodded. "Groundskeeper at the bowls club. Been doing it for around six months."

"Have you spotted him yet?"

"That's him working the scoreboard," Walker said, knowing there was no point in lying to her. "But you better not go scaring him off."

"Wouldn't dream of it." Bernie tilted her head to one side. "Look, there's no need for us to have a barny. Why don't we join forces today? We can interview Cammy at the same time, like good cop and much better PI."

"You make it sound so tempting," Walker grimaced.

"I'm not kidding. I've just been chatting to your boss."

"Ferguson?" Walker blinked. He couldn't quite imagine how the uptight DI would cope if he came face to face with Bernie Paterson.

"No, the real brains. Macleod."

"You weren't hassling him, were you? He's only just back at work."

"Seemed strong enough to me," Bernie shrugged. "Anyway, he accepted that the WWC had as much info on this case as you lot did."

"He said that did he?"

"Yep. And he didn't tell me not to help you, so why not give it a shot?"

It was getting very hot. A bead of sweat ran down Walker's temple and settled on his collar.

"Fine. It's too hot to argue. But you let me take the lead in the interview."

"Of course," Bernie replied.

They were saved from making any small talk by the ringing of a large bell.

"Half time," Walker told her. "Let's go and find our man."

Cammy Venny was still sitting next to the scoreboard only now he had pulled out a vape pen and was puffing vanilla steam into the air. Walker just knew that Bernie was going to start a mini lecture about the dangers of vaping, so he made sure to step in front of her and hold out his badge.

"Could I have a quick word, Mr Venny?"

"Can I stop you?" Venny wheezed out a laugh. He was maybe sixty years old, skin browned from working outside and a little pot belly that suggested he liked the odd beer to go with his vape.

"My name is Sergeant Walker and this is Bernadette Paterson. We would like to speak to you about Gavin Eyre."

"I saw he'd turned up," the man shrugged. "I'm afraid I'm not involved in that world anymore."

"Seems like quite a nice little job for you here," Bernie said.

Cammy nodded. "Beats litter picking."

"It was benefit fraud, wasn't it, that you were sent down for last time."

He shuffled his feet. "Aye. Only nicked a few grand. It's not like it's easy for someone like me to get a job."

Walker was glad that Mary wasn't there or she might have fallen for the sob story. Bernie on the other hand looked like she would have quite happily thrown the man back in jail.

"You need to work for your opportunities," the woman told Cammy. "But at least you've got something good going here. I hope you appreciate it."

"I do. The boss has said he might even sort something out for me when I've finished my sentence. A janitor type thing. I don't mind a bit of hard work."

"What sort of work were you doing back in nineteen ninety-four?" Walker asked.

"You'll have seen my record so you already know."

Nearby a woman was handing out glasses of iced water and a bluetit flickered about in Walker's peripheral vision. It was an oddly peaceful place to be discussing murder.

"Have you any idea what Gavin was involved in before he disappeared," Walker asked. He was getting tired of the man's evasions.

Cammy rubbed at his chin. "When was this again?"

"April nineteen ninety-four."

"That was just when my missus started to get sick. It was cancer, you see. She'd already had it once and then it came back. And the treatment back then was brutal. She was dead within a year."

"Sorry to hear it."

"No you're not," Cammy said, but he didn't seem to mind. "What I'm telling you is, I stepped away from all the jobs around then. Jen needed me to look after her. So I don't have a clue what anyone was getting up to, including Gavin Eyre."

"All right."

"Do you have any idea why someone might have wanted to kill him?" Bernie asked.

"He was a bit of a chancer," Cammy told them. "A bit cocky, I suppose. Thought he knew everything even though he was just a young lad. There were plenty of people around then that wouldn't take it well if you tried to play the big man. I reckon someone lost their temper with him and that was it."

"And you wouldn't have any idea who might have done it?"

Another shrug. "Like I said, could have been anyone."

Bernie tried a few more questions, but only received short, sullen answers. They ended up leaving the man when the players came back out.

"That was a bloody waste of time," Bernie said. "Another criminal from the nineties who saw nothing and did nothing. Can't you take him into the station and give him a beating to make him talk?"

Walker hoped she was joking.

"I'm just as frustrated as you are," he told her. "If we don't get a lead on this case they'll send me back to the college."

"And away from Mary," Bernie reminded him.

"Yeah. I suppose you wouldn't mind that," Walker said.

"I have come to the reluctant conclusion that Mary Plunkett seems to love you. Despite your obvious failings, number one being your choice of profession."

"Right."

"So it would probably be for the best if you stuck around.

Let's make a deal: we work this case together. I said the same to Macleod. It's in your interests and mine to find out who killed Gavin Eyre."

Walker couldn't help but smile. "And what happens when our interests don't align?"

"Then I'll happily wave you goodbye."

Chapter 27: Bernie

The curtains were drawn at Mrs Eyre's house even though it was the middle of the day. Bernie understood why the woman might want to hide away from the world, but it wasn't going to stop the investigations of the WWC.

"Are you sure we shouldn't bring Walker," Mary whispered. "I'm not sure that we should be going in alone."

"What, you think she's going to attack us with the Reader's Digest?" Bernie banged on the door. "I reckon we'll be okay."

"Yes, but –"

"But nothing. Look, you've got a good hunch here, and I'm willing to bet it's on the nose, but we've no evidence to back it up. The police would laugh us out of the station. We'll do this as it should be done: me, you and a vulnerable elderly lady in her own house."

"Christ," Mary moaned, then fell silent.

Bernie thumped on the door one more time.

"I don't want to speak to you," Mrs Eyre said from the other side of the frosted glass. "I want to be left alone."

"I want Chris Hemsworth in a bucket of ice-cream," Bernie yelled back, "but we can't all have what we want, can we now?"

Mrs Eyre blinked. "Who the hell are you?"

"This is my partner, Bernadette Paterson," Mary explained. "And I really think it's best if you let us in. She's not the sort of person it's safe to leave on the doorstep."

Whether out of fear or confusion, Mrs Eyre opened the door and moved back to allow them into the house.

The living room was small and had that stale smell that you get when you keep the curtains closed. The television was on, blaring some dreadful daytime TV thing. Bernie picked up the remote control and switched it off.

"Hey!" Mary and Mrs Eyre called out simultaneously.

"This is an important chat," Bernie said, giving Mary a glare. "I think you're going to want to pay attention, Mrs Eyre."

The woman glowered at her.

"My friend Mary here is a very clever lady."

"I am?"

"Yes. But her mind works in a quite peculiar way."

"Oh."

"Me, I go for things straight on. Either I know the answer or I don't. But Mary here, she works differently."

Bernie looked to Mary, who took up the narrative.

"That's right," Mary cleared her throat. "I've been speaking to a lot of people about the past. And one of the things I wanted to find out about was Gavin's childhood."

"You had no right," Mrs Eyre snapped. "What's that got to do with anything?"

"That's the problem with murder cases, I'm afraid," Mary said, her tone kindly. "You never know what's relevant or not. I'm sure the police have already asked you about the post mortem. About the injuries they found on Gavin's body. The ones from when he was a kid."

"I don't... I don't know anything about it."

Mary let out a laugh at that one. "Oh come on now. I'm a mother, remember? You know when your child sneezes, let alone breaks a rib. You must have known all about it, Mrs Eyre."

The woman said nothing, but her lips were pressed together so firmly that they were white.

"And I'm not here to judge. I'm willing to bet you had a few broken ribs of your own. Everything we've learned about Reggie Eyre suggests he was a violent drunk, the nastiest sort of criminal. And I've seen enough battered women to know that it feels like you can't escape it."

"He said he'd take the kids," Mrs Eyre said, so quiet it was almost in a whisper.

"Aye, they often do that," Bernie told her. "Beat you and lie to you until you have nowhere to turn."

"We applied for Reggie's death certificate," Mary said. "He died when Gavin was fourteen, is that right?"

Mrs Eyre nodded.

"And the cause of death was heart failure. Well, as Bernie could tell you, we all die of heart failure in the end, right? So that didn't tell us much. But I kept thinking about how nervous you were, about the police and about me being in the house. It felt like you had something to hide."

Mrs Eyre kept silent.

"And I tracked down a girl that Gavin was seeing. Louise Steele, I'm not sure if he mentioned her? But she said something about being afraid of Gavin's family. But it wasn't his father or his brother that she mentioned. It was you. You see, Gavin had got drunk one day and told her something. He told her that he thought his mother might have killed his father."

"Rubbish," Mrs Eyre said, but she would have been a dreadful poker player. Her fingers clutched at her knees.

"We could ask Francis about it," Bernie said, turning the screw. "He would have been eighteen at the time. He must have suspected what happened."

"Don't you dare!" Mrs Eyre's voice began to waver.

Mary gave a sharp nod, as if that was confirmation enough. "You tell us then, Mrs Eyre. It's been eating you up for more than thirty years. Time to tell us all about it."

For a moment Bernie thought the Mary Plunkett magic hadn't worked this time. Then Mrs Eyre began to talk.

"The last time was the worst. Gavin was eight years old and Freddie just went for him. I was sure that he'd broken the kid's ribs, but he wouldn't let me take him to the doctors. That boy sobbed for days, but sort of quiet-like. That's how my boys learned to cry. Silently, so that it didn't make anyone angrier. Can you imagine that?"

Even Bernie couldn't think of anything to say, but luckily the words were flowing out of Mrs Eyre now like a whole river of pain.

"I wanted to leave so badly, but where would we go? I wasn't going to have the kids living on the streets. Everyone looking at me like I was scum. So I made a deal with Freddie. If he never hit the lad again I wouldn't tell anyone about him thumping Gavin so bad. And for six years, he didn't."

Mrs Eyre chewed the inside of her lip. "And then the boys turned into teenagers and Gavin started getting more cheeky. Pushing his dad, getting up in his face, like. And then Francis would stick up for him and the arguing would start. And I would look at Freddie's red cheeks and I knew it was just a matter of time before it happened again."

She took a deep breath.

"And I realised that no one was going to come and save us. No one was going to make it better. And I'd seen the way Francis had looked at his father when he hurt Gavin. The total hatred. And I knew that if I didn't do something, then Francis was going to kill his father."

"Francis didn't do it though, did he," Bernie said, the woman's voice soft for once.

"No. Like I keep telling you lot and those stupid coppers, my Francis never killed anyone."

"But someone else did, am I right?" Bernie continued. "Someone wanted to save Francis from having to do it."

"That's right. Gavin had been caught smoking after school. Smoking! After all the things that Freddie got up to, he had a nerve to be mad about a wee cigarette. But he was. So mad he could hardly speak. Well, he was on these blood pressure tablets anyway, and you could see his face getting redder and redder. And when he asked for a glass of whiskey, I put some of the tablets in his drink. When he went to sleep, he never woke up."

The only sound was the clock on the mantel ticking.

"If you think I'm going to start bawling over it then you're wrong. That man wasn't worth any tears." Despite her words, Bernie could see the woman's chin begin to wobble.

"If you'd gone to the police," Mary piped up, "maybe explained that it was self-defence…"

She trailed off. Bernie was itching to get out of there. They weren't going to get anything else out of the woman now that she had slumped back on the sofa, exhausted by her confession.

"Do you swear to us that your husband's death had nothing to do with Gavin's murder?" Bernie asked her.

"Of course it didn't."

"Gavin might have found out about it," Bernie said, knowing she needed to keep pushing until she was sure. "He might have been upset that you killed his father. Maybe he confronted you and you hit him. Something like that."

"Nothing like that. Gavin never said it, but he was happy that his father wasn't around any more. Jesus, you know what Freddie did to him. Not a single person on this earth missed that man after he was gone."

"All right. We better get going," Bernie said, moving towards the door.

"I suppose you'll tell those police officers all about it," Mrs Eyre said, her head hanging low.

"Let them do their own investigating," Bernie said firmly. "Don't see why we should be doing it for them."

Mrs Eyre raised her eyebrows but didn't reply. They left her still sitting on the sofa, staring at the blank screen of the TV.

Bernie knew something was wrong when they got back in the car and Mary had gone silent. Normally the woman prattled on continuously, so the chill in the air alerted even Bernie's underdeveloped people skills.

"Something wrong?"

"No," Mary replied, but she was staring out of the window. Bernie reckoned she knew what the problem was.

"You think we should be reporting her to the police?"

"It's a murder isn't it?" Sure enough, Mary's jaw was tight with tension. "If she killed her husband then there should be justice."

Bernie glared at the woman. "Justice? What, put that old woman in jail because she stood up to the man that had been beating her up for years? You think that's justice?"

"I just think that the court should decide. A jury. Isn't that the point?"

"I decide," Bernie said, and she was barely managing to control her temper. "Haven't you realised that yet? Our job is to work around the police, not with them. Or have you forgotten that?"

Mary's eyes dropped to the floor. "No. But…"

"But me no buts," Bernie replied, remembering a phrase from her mother of all people. "You sleep on it tonight. I reckon you'll agree with me in the morning."

Mary nodded and a little of the tension leeched out of the car.

"So where do we go from here?" Mary asked.

"Back to the start, I reckon. Back to nineteen ninety-four."

"Pity we don't have the Tardis," Mary said. "Or a Delorean for that matter."

"Is that some sort of fancy cocktail I don't know about?"

"Never mind," Mary replied.

Chapter 28: Liz

There was a weird atmosphere in the WWC meeting on Monday night and Liz was not enjoying it one bit. They were in Annie McGillivray's house and despite the copious amount of pastries that Mary had brought with her, the woman's expression was sour. Bernie had told Liz about what had happened with Mrs Eyre. In the moment, Liz wasn't sure which of the other two she would have supported. She shared Mary's concern that a murder was going unpunished, but she could also see Bernie's point of view. Why bring the family more misery when it wouldn't make a difference?

Of course, part of the problem was Bernie herself. She hadn't spared Mrs Eyre out of a heartfelt compassion, although Liz knew that her friend was occasionally capable of that. No, Liz knew fine well that Bernie had decided she should be the one to pass judgement and that was that. It was no wonder that Mary was feeling a little peeved.

"I'll start shall I," Liz said, cutting through the silence. "I've had some movement on the Hart inheritance case."

"Excellent."

"It's not quite the good news we were hoping for. You remember that I went to see Caron Gibson who we thought was a distant relative of the deceased?"

Bernie and Mary nodded.

"Well, Mrs Gibson said she was going to look out some birth certificates that we could use for proof of inheritance. There was a box of old papers, apparently, that had been left in her loft after her mother died. So Mrs Gibson goes up into the loft and starts rooting through the paperwork. And she found her own birth certificate. The real one, not the doctored one her mother had given her."

"Oh no," Mary raised her hands in front of her mouth.

"Oh yes. The father's name was not the one that she expected. Turns out that Caron's biological father was in fact the local milk delivery man, not the man that she knew for fifty years or so."

"Whoops," Bernie said.

"Whoops indeed. Both of her parents are dead, by the way, so it's not like they could explain themselves. And so Caron went off to see her oldest cousin Shirley who told her that everyone in the family knew, it was an open secret and she couldn't understand why Caron was so upset about it. Then Caron punched Shirley on the nose."

Mary's eyes were huge and she whistled in a gasp.

"This all sounds… suboptimal," Bernie said, master of the understatement as usual.

Liz continued. "Yeah. This had all happened in the beer garden of the local pub, by the way. While a tribute act was singing the hits of Boy George with an acoustic guitar. The first I heard about it was when Caron called me after they released her from the police station. Thankfully the cousin isn't going to press charges and Caron has got off with a Caution."

Bernie frowned. "But what does that mean for the inheritance? I mean, if the birth certificate has been changed then she won't inherit, right?"

"Nope. The family line goes down the mother's side. Caron will still get the cash, and now that I've signed up all of her cousins, including the one with the broken nose, we should get our cut as well."

This won her genuine smiles from her friends.

"Excellent," Bernie leaned back in her chair. "You did good work on that one."

"Thanks," Liz said, warmed by the praise, especially as Bernie wasn't known for giving it out often.

"Unfortunately, the news on Gavin Eyre is not quite so rosy. After our little visit to the Eyre household, we seem to be back at square one with the case," Bernie said, pulling up the spreadsheet on her laptop. "Mrs Eyre had nothing to do with her son's death, and we don't seem to be much closer to finding who did."

"We haven't worked out who this woman was he was shagging," Mary reminded them. "I'm sure she must know something. Could you ask Francis about her?"

"I'll certainly try, but he's not answering the phone at the moment. We need to keep going on our other leads. I'm not going to let the coppers beat us on this one," Bernie said. "Not when we're so close to finding out what really happened to Gavin."

Mary shifted in her seat. "Do you think that maybe it's so important to you because you feel you owe it to eighteen year old Bernie? Like, you can let her know that she was right all along."

"Well thanks, Dr Phil, for your startling psychological insight."

Liz's tone was a warning. "Bernie, play nice."

"What? We're here to solve a murder not for a therapy session."

"Sorry I spoke," Mary said, slumping into sulky silence.

Liz wished that Bernie would at least pretend to consider other people's feelings, but she was incapable of it. Her inability to be anything other than her true self was both her worst and her best quality.

"I've been working through this list of gangsters," Liz said, trying to get their attention back to the case. "And I wasn't getting anywhere with them until I remembered that the woman from the paper, Laney Blackwell. I thought she might know at least some of the names and when I sent her an email, she came up trumps. Let me read you what she sent me back."

Liz brought up the email on her phone.

Dear Ms Okoro,

Sorry I haven't been in touch. There was a flood at the Gala day on Thursday and three local councillors got swept into the river. They had to cling onto a discarded shopping trolley until the fire brigade rescued them, so as you can imagine the pictures have gone national.

I didn't think I had anything for you anyway, not until you mentioned your list of names of local 'characters'. They brought back some memories! It really was the Wild West here back then. But when I saw the name Starling it started the old neurons firing. I remembered that in early ninety-four there was a big wedding with Starling's sister who got married to a local garage owner. The reason it made the papers was that it was a real 'new money' event. It was reported they spent twenty thousand, which as you can imagine was a huge amount back then. There were eyebrows raised as well because the lady had been divorced and was now getting married in the Cathedral. Anyway, I searched through the archives and I found this photograph of the day. You might find it interesting!

Remember you owe me an exclusive

LB.

Bernie and Mary crowded around to see the photo. It was the typical picture of the bridal couple in front of the church, groom looking awkward and bride beaming at the attention. But in the background were a group of men that looked familiar. At the far right was Gavin Eyre, looking young and full of life.

"That's Starling there, next to the bride," Bernie said. "And Cammy Venny next to him."

"Who's the woman in between them? She's standing close to Gavin?"

"I'm not sure," Bernie said. "They look like they're having a cosy wee chat though, don't they?"

"It could be nothing," Mary said, staring at the picture.

"But it could be something."

"True."

"I'll ask Francis who she is," Bernie said. "Once I can get hold of him."

"I'm going to message Starling," Liz added. "If it was his sister's wedding then he's more likely to know the guests. And I haven't set the HMRC on him yet, so he might even give us an answer."

"Excellent," Bernie replied. "Mary, pop the kettle on won't you?"

Mary narrowed her eyes but went through to the kitchen as requested. Liz wondered if she should warn Bernie that she was irritating their friend, but then what was the point? She probably already knew.

Chapter 29: Mary

Make the bloody tea, Mary said to herself as she filled up the kettle. Oh yes, I'm meant to be a full partner now, but I still have to make the bloody tea. The truth was, she was normally quite happy to make the tea. Bernie was one of those people that if you asked for two sugars they would only put one in, as if they were doing you a favour. At least this way she could get it nice and syrupy herself. But she was in a bad mood with Bernie, so everything the woman said was irritating her.

The thing was, once she'd had time to think about it, she agreed with Bernie that prosecuting Mrs Eyre would be no good for anyone. But it was the fact that her supposed partner hadn't even considered that her opinion might be valid, that was what was getting on her nerves.

And the Gavin Eyre case wasn't helping. Mary had been certain when they'd followed up on Gavin's girlfriend and his mystery woman that they would prove the lead to take them to his killer, but it had all fizzled out into nothing. To top it all off, Walker had phoned her to say that unless something changed on the case today he would be back in Tulliallan for the rest of the month.

She grabbed the mugs of tea and went back into the living room to hear Bernie explaining her plans to Liz.

"I want to do a reconstruction," Bernie was saying. "Go up to the reservoir, every one of us. I want to see what it's like up there. It's not like the pub or his house or anything. Places like that don't change much in thirty years."

"All right, if you think it'll help," Liz replied. "When were you thinking?"

"Tomorrow afternoon."

"Ah," Mary said, her heart falling.

Bernie swivelled around so that she could look the woman in the eyes. "If we don't do something we're going to let this case slip through our fingers. The reconstruction is not optional."

Mary raised her hand.

"What? You're not in school," Bernie said. She seemed to be even tetchier than usual today. "Just ask your question."

"I'm sorry but I can't make it. It's school sports day. I never miss it."

"What, watching the kids trip up over their own feet? I'm sure they can spare you this once."

"I just don't think –"

"I need you there," Bernie said.

Mary swallowed. "I'm sorry Bernie but it's just not possible. I've never missed a sports day and I won't ever miss one. The kids deserve a parent there and they've only got me."

"Ridiculous," Bernie said.

"I think that she's got a point, Berns," Liz said, trying to intervene. "I mean, it is important."

"What, watching little Johnny win the three-legged race will be the highlight of his childhood, will it," Bernie said in her most condescending tone. "If that's the case then you'd better take a look at yourself."

Mary felt her lip start to tremble. "I'm really not interested in your opinion," she said. "I've made up my mind and I won't be going to the reconstruction. My kids are more important."

"More important than catching a murderer?"

"Yes."

"Fine then," Bernie said.

There was a horrible, awkward silence and Mary felt like bursting into tears. Liz changed the subject and started talking about the business accounts but Bernie continued to glare at her, and Mary couldn't stomach the conversation. A few minutes later she said she had to get going and grabbed her coat. No one asked her to stay.

Chapter 30: Walker

When Walker arrived for his shift on Tuesday, McNicholl was laughing with Rav at the coffee machine. They were comparing how bad their local football teams were. McNicholl had said the fatal words of 'Greenock Morton' and that had set Rav off in a fit of amusement.

"You're in a good mood," Walker told them.

"Yep," Rav replied, "not only is our mentor a supporter of the roughest football team in Scotland, but it looks like I was wrong about this case being dead."

"What do you mean"

"Ferguson arrested Francis Eyre this morning," McNicholl said.

Walker's jaw dropped. "Bloody hell. Bernie's going to go mental."

"What's a Bernie?" McNicholl asked, her face puzzled.

"Never mind. What was the evidence for the arrest?"

"It all came back to those cars. Ferguson was looking at who kept dumping them in the river. He wasn't getting very far, until he spoke to this guy, Ari Jackson. He runs a chain of garages, but he used to be a scrap dealer back in the day. He says that there was a bunch of kids that used to steal cars to order, they would strip them of the parts and then dump them.

And guess who was in charge of it all?"

"Francis?"

"Yep."

"But they only have this guy Jackson's word for it, right?"

McNicholl shook her head. "They got a DNA match on one of the other cars from the reservoir. A clump of hair caught in the door matches Francis. Nothing on the car with Gavin's body in it, but it puts Francis at the scene."

Walker nodded. It was enough to get an arrest warrant at least.

"They are going to question him in a minute," Rav told him. "If you cosy up to your pal DI Macleod then he might let us watch."

Walker wasn't even offended by Rav's tone. "Sure. Got to be worth a try."

He didn't manage to find Macleod, but he did bump into DI Ferguson just before he was about to go into the interview room.

"I was wondering if Rav and I might be able to observe, sir. It would be great for us to see how an interview is conducted in these circumstances."

Ferguson adjusted his glasses. "I suppose it would look good on your learning plan. Sure, why not? Tell Sergeant Sangar to meet you in the observation room."

Walker collected up his colleague and went to stand in the

room just along the corridor from the interview room. McNicoll invited herself along too. This sort of breakthrough in a case always drew in a crowd. At the last moment, the door opened to admit Macleod, who tilted his head to them in recognition.

In the old days, they would have been able to stare at the suspect through a one-way mirror. Nowadays the same effect was achieved through a pair of cameras showing on large monitors. It wasn't quite as fun, but that was policing for you. They watched as Francis Eyre was led into the interview room along with a solicitor. His legal advisor was in her thirties with braided black hair and an electric blue suit. Her colourful attire only accentuated the grey tone of Francis Eyre's skin and his hang-dog expression.

Ferguson and a Detective Constable that Walker didn't recognise sat down opposite them. Each person identified themselves for the tape, which is how he learned that the DC's name was Hunter.

There were the usual legal definitions and introductions before Ferguson got started on the interview proper.

"We have arrested you in connection with the abduction and wrongful death of Gavin Eyre in nineteen ninety-four. Do you understand?"

Francis was certainly no newcomer to a police interrogation. He said his name and his date of birth, but apart from that it was 'no comment' all the way. It might have made for a boring watch, but Walker was interested to see just what evidence DI Ferguson had collected.

As if Ferguson had felt Walker's impatience, the DI brought out some photographs to show his suspect. These were images of the cars found in Invergryff reservoir.

"All these cars were stolen within half a mile of your pub. And most interesting to me is that we found your DNA on one of these cars, Francis. This grey one here. And it was dumped almost touching distance from the one that we discovered your brother's body in."

"No comment."

Ferguson's jaw clenched, but he kept going through the photos. He placed the picture of the red Ford Escort in front of Francis. "This car, the one your brother was found in was stolen just around the corner from where the others were taken. On Forth Avenue."

Up until this moment, Francis had looked more bored than anything else. But now he stared at the Inspector.

"Did you say Forth Avenue?"

"Yes."

Francis sucked at his teeth. "Can't have been me. Or any of my lads neither. Forth Avenue is over the council line. It's part of Greater Glasgow."

It was Ferguson's turn to frown, an expression that was echoed in the observation room.

"What's with the geography lesson?" Rav asked, but no one had an answer.

In the interview room, however, Francis was already explaining himself.

"I'm not saying that I was into getting rid of any of these cars or anything... But if I had been, my patch was just Renfrewshire, see? I was always a local boy, and I knew to keep to my place. Some of these Glasgow lads, they were pretty bloody strict about whose territory was whose. I would never have nicked a car from Forth Avenue. Not if I wanted to keep both my kneecaps."

"Crap," Macleod said. Walker felt the same way. DI Ferguson had kept his face neutral, but everyone could tell that the rest of the interview would just be going through the motions. Francis was bright enough for a career criminal, but he wasn't the sort to make up something like that. Not when he knew it could easily be checked.

The interview continued, but everyone already knew the outcome. Francis Eyre hadn't killed his brother.

Chapter 31: Bernie

On Tuesday morning, Bernie didn't feel like visiting Mary but Liz had told her to be nice. In fact, what Liz Okoro had texted was:

You better damn well apologise to Mary. You know she's the best investigator of the lot of us and if she leaves because you're being a pain in the arse I'll never forgive you.

If Bernie was honest, she still didn't see what she had done wrong. Sports day was stupid, and their reconstruction of the crime was clearly much more important. But with two out of the three WWC members mad at her, it meant that the organisation would not be functioning at peak efficiency. And that more than anything else persuaded her to knock on Mary's door that morning.

Unfortunately, just before she arrived at Mary's house she got a text message that drove all thoughts of an apology from her mind. Instead, she met Mary at the door with a scowl.

"Your bloody boyfriend!"

"What's he done now?" Mary asked. She was wearing a hoodie with 'Don't trust meerkats in dinner jackets' written on it, for some unfathomable reason.

"They've arrested Francis Eyre."

"What?" Mary's eyes goggled at her.

"Yep, my contact Mrs Battaglia who works there as a cleaner spotted them taking him into the station this afternoon. And I'm going to have to buy her a bag of doughnuts for giving me the information."

"They must have a reason to arrest him," Mary reminded her.

"Oh, they always have some sort of reason. But they can't see what is plain to everyone else. That Francis Eyre was just like his mother."

Mary frowned. "What do you mean by that?"

"I mean that Mrs Eyre would do anything in the world to protect Gavin. We know that she even killed her husband, just to save the boy. And Francis grew up with that model. He saw his father beat his brother and he would have done anything to save him too. So the idea that he killed Gavin is simply impossible."

Mary said nothing, which irritated Bernie further. She was far too quick to believe in the intelligence of the local constabulary. Bernie on the other hand had quite a different opinion of the boys in Invergryff Police Station.

"What are you going to do about it?" Mary asked.

"My first thought was to go down there and knock some heads together. But what would be the point? They'll need to learn their mistake in their own time. So what we'll do is we'll keep working through this case. We're getting closer now, I can smell it."

This time, Mary nodded her agreement. "It does feel like we're getting close. I think we've got a good sense of what was going on in Gavin's head at the time of his death."

"Why don't you talk me through it," Bernie said. As much as Mary Plunkett drove her crazy, the woman's sideways way of looking at the world often brought up ideas that Bernie herself would never have considered.

"All right. In the days before his death, we know that some things had changed for Gavin," Mary said, leaning her head on her chin. "Firstly, his relationship. Louise told us that she broke up with him not long before he disappeared, but the reason for this was that she thought he was seeing someone else. And now we know that he was using the care home as a wee love nest to meet someone there. And this was after Louise had left, so it wasn't her."

"Yep, we certainly need to consider the new woman angle," Bernie nodded. "I wish we knew who she was."

"I do too," Mary said. "Because it seems to me that there might be a connection with whatever was going on with his criminal connections. There was a rumour that Gavin was going to come into some money. Was this related to the new girlfriend? Or some sort of dodgy business deal."

"That's where we hit a bit of a wall," Bernie said, her mood falling. "None of those old gangsters are going to admit to us that Gavin was working on a job for them. Especially if it went wrong."

"Who can we put pressure on?" Mary asked. "Is there anyone we haven't tracked down yet?"

"MacCulloch," Bernie answered. "He's in a care home now over in Govan. I phoned them up but it's dementia. Barely knows his own name, poor sod."

"Did he have a wife? Anyone we can talk to?"

"I didn't follow it up," Bernie said, realising she should have done. "I'll give the care home another call."

"Good. I'll see you later, then," Mary said, a little stiffly.

The door shut and Bernie turned back to the car. She didn't have time to soothe any hurt feelings right now, even if it did unsettle her a little that Mary was still bent out of shape. By the time Bernie got back to the car her mind was firmly back on the case. She sent off an email to the care home and then started the car.

After she left Mary's place, Bernie went to pick up Liz for the reconstruction. She wasn't too happy when she pulled up at Liz's house and saw her friend walking towards her with a buggy on one arm and a baby on the other.

"Are you bringing Issy?" Bernie said.

"Yep. My mum was meant to be babysitting, but she's off on some protest march. Can't remember if it's climate change or war in the Middle East this time."

"Selfish," Bernie shook her head. "At least it'll be a nice walk in the woods for the little one."

"That's what I figured," Liz said, strapping a gurgling Isioma into her car seat.

It was the perfect weather for a Scottish walk in the woods: a light drizzle that turned the paths slick with mud. By the time they had parked up in a layby and stared out at the rain, Bernie was already regretting her mission.

"I come up here for runs sometimes," she explained to Liz. "This is the closest place to park near the reservoir. Unless you're driving into it, of course."

"Of course. Shall we go?"

They manoeuvred Issy into the buggy, made sure her rain cover was secured and walked through the gate towards the woods.

"My shoes are going to be ruined," Liz grumbled.

"Should have brought your hiking boots," Bernie said, lifting her foot to show her own, much more appropriate footwear.

"Whatever gave you the impression that I owned hiking boots," Liz said, wiping some grey mud from the side of her smart leather brogues.

Bernie was already scouting out the route around them. They had to bring the cars this way, she explained as they walked. "This is the only gate wide enough to admit a car and if they'd driven through a fence someone would have noticed."

They rounded another bend and the reservoir appeared before them. It was a sorry sight. Bernie had seen it before it had been drained and it had been pleasant enough, even if there was fly tipping and tangles of brambles dotted around it. But now that it had been drained it was just a muddy hollow with no redeeming features.

"What a mess," Liz said and Bernie had to agree.

"Are they going to fill it up again?"

"No idea."

What a miserable place to be your grave for thirty years. Bernie wasn't the sentimental type, and she knew fine well that wherever the living presence of Gavin Eyre was now, it was nowhere near this patch of mud. But if she wasn't prone to sympathy for others, she could certainly feel pure rage on their behalf.

"I'll solve this one if it kills me," Bernie whispered to herself.

They walked back to the car in thoughtful silence.

"If nothing else, Isioma enjoyed her walk," Liz said, checking on the little one who was now fast asleep in the buggy.

"It is not a walk if she's been sitting down the whole time. Anyway, it has confirmed something for me," Bernie said as they walked back to the car. "No way would you just happen upon this place to dump a body. There are a hundred spots between here and Invergryff where you could drive a car off the road and into the woods. Someone knew this was the perfect spot."

"Then maybe the police are right about Francis," Liz suggested. "He dumped the other cars."

"It wasn't him," Bernie told her. "No matter what those idiots at the station think. Oh, I'm sure they dumped the cars. But he wasn't acting alone, was he? He was part of a gang of people getting rid of those stolen motors. We need to get those names."

"Do you reckon Francis will give you them?"

"He might need a little persuading," Bernie admitted. "But I know how to get to him."

"Really?"

"Yeah. I'll just threaten to knee him in the bollocks again."

"You're funny," Liz said.

Bernie couldn't see the joke.

Chapter 32: Liz

Liz wasn't sure if she should be proud or worried about the current state of the living room walls. The Gangsta Wall Chart™ had taken over three walls. It was colour-coded, had grainy pictures pinned up from old newspaper articles and the odd embellishment in crayon by her younger child.

"It's incredible," Dave told Sean, giving him a high five. Liz was glad that she had shown Dave the wall chart privately before Sean was there, because her husband's first reaction hadn't been nearly so positive.

"Pity we can't submit it to the school for a project," Liz told her son. "Maybe you could recreate the concept another time with something less…"

"Murdery?" Dave suggested.

"Exactly. Still, it's a work of art." Liz moved closer. "What's this section here?"

"Oh, Bernie gave me a call about that Cammy guy, so I added him in. He's in my B team, not as high up as the others."

"Bernie called you?"

"Yeah."

Liz wasn't too sure how she felt about that. It was one thing for Sean to be giving her a hand, but it seemed like an escalation for Bernie to be getting him further involved. Apart from anything else, he might need paying.

"What's this note next to him; 'dead wife'?"

"His wife had cancer or something. That's why he wasn't involved so much when Gavin disappeared. That's what he told Bernie anyway."

"Huh. I might double-check that one." It was hard to believe that the pretty woman that Liz had seen in the wedding photo had died just a few months later.

"What have you got on MacCulloch?" Liz asked. "Bernie reckons he's in a care home now."

"Ooh, he's a good one," Sean said, hopping over to the right-hand side of the wall. "They called him the Southside Slasher."

"Nice. I don't suppose he had a habit of killing people and dumping their bodies in cars?"

"Don't know. He was famous for giving people the Glasgow smile. You know, where they cut the mouth and –"

"Maybe we should leave it there for now," Liz said, catching Dave's expression out of the corner of her eye.

"Come on, footie time," Dave said, ushering Sean out into the garden. Of course, Isioma demanded to come too, so in a few moments Liz was left alone with the wall of infamy.

Liz folded her arms and stared at the wall. Somewhere on here was the reason that Gavin Eyre ended his days submerged in a car boot. She just had to find it.

As if on cue, her phone rang.

"Hey, you got a minute?" Bernie asked.

"Sure."

"Like I said to you earlier, I've been looking at this MacCulloch character."

"So have we. I hope you know that my son is now obsessed with true crime."

"Sensible boy. Now, I've got a possible contact for MacCulloch's son. His name is James and he lives in Glasgow, just over the river in Partick. Reckon you could drive over there? I'd do it myself but I've already got an appointment for this afternoon."

"All right," Liz said, knowing that Dave would moan about missing his golf game to watch the kids, but also knowing that she didn't particularly care.

After only a mild verbal altercation with her husband, Liz drove over to Glasgow and found the address that Bernie had given her. She had to circle around for a few minutes before she found a parking space near the tenement flat where James MacCulloch lived.

Glasgow tenements were a funny thing. A few streets away in posh Hyndland, a flat in a building like this would cost you several hundred thousand pounds. MacCulloch's building, however, was at the dodgier end of Partick, where the bottom floor was occupied by vape stores and charity shops and the flats above looked distinctly run down.

The man who opened the door looked to be around the same age as Liz. He had shaved his head, and he had a muscular, wiry physique. He was also very nervous, his hands fidgeting as he spoke.

"I'm just about to go out."

There was the distinct smell of weed.

"I won't be long."

"The woman on the phone said you'd give me fifty quid if I talked to you about my dad."

"I think she said it would be twenty," Liz said, holding out the note that was their standard offering in these situations. MacCulloch looked about to argue, then he snatched it out of her hand.

"Fine."

Liz walked into the flat and immediately promised herself not to touch any of the surfaces. There was a general griminess about the place that made her want to get the bleach out.

"I wanted to talk to you about your father," Liz told him.

"Doesn't even remember his own name now, poor old sod."

Liz wondered how the child of someone that had once owned half the businesses in Govan was living in a nasty little place like this. But she didn't have the time to find out.

"We're investigating the death of Gavin Eyre. I know that he sometimes did work for your dad back in the nineties."

"Bloody disgrace that," James said. His eyes flicked around the room as if he couldn't settle on anything. "Those cops never even tried to find him."

"Did you know Gavin?"

"Aye. He was a few years older than me. I kind of looked up to him."

"You did?"

"He was nice to me. Bought me ciggies sometimes."

"Then you'll want to help us find out who killed him," Liz told him.

"Don't see how I can be any help. Like I said, I was just a dumb kid."

"I want to know who was working with your dad when Gavin was about. Anyone that might have fallen out with him, or been angry with him about something."

"Well, I never saw anything like that. But I can give you the names of the people hanging around back then. For another twenty quid."

Liz rolled her eyes, but handed him another twenty. "That's your lot though."

James popped it into his pocket. "All right, so I can tell you the names because most of these guys are dead or in some care home like my dad. There was Billy Cooper, Rob Bremner and Darryn Gallacher. They were like Dad's deputies, you get me?

All dead apart from Darryn Gallacher and he moved to Newcastle years ago, so I've no idea if he's alive or not. I remember Gavin hanging around with Andy Hay a bit. Andy was the money guy and I think Gavin liked the idea of getting into that work. But it didn't happen."

"Why not?"

James laughed. "He was crap at maths. Dad wasn't a charity case. If you couldn't do the job you were out on your ear. Anyway, Andy Hay left the business, I think he set up a garage or something. And then there were the sort of outside guys. The ones that were never really part of the team but Dad would use them if he was stuck. Guys like Cammy and Wee Tam."

"Would that be Cammy Venny?" Liz asked, noting that the name had come up before.

"Aye. I remember him because he was a bit of a pity case." MacCulloch saw Liz look puzzled. "What I mean is, Dad felt sorry for Cammy. I mean, everyone did. His wife got sick, you know? Dad even gave him a car."

"He did?"

"Aye. It was nicked, of course, but he still got a bit of use out of it. Nice little red Ford."

Liz's heart started to beat faster. "You're sure it was red?"

"Yes. I've always liked cars. Used to love them until I lost my license."

"And Cammy had a red Ford Escort?"

MacCulloch looked up at the excited note in her voice. "Aye. Does that get me another twenty?"

"No," Liz said. "But thanks for the info."

She left the flat not just feeling relieved at getting some fresh air, but with the tantalising idea that she might be getting somewhere.

As she walked down the communal stairway a guy pushed past her. The man who was wearing a hoodie pulled low over his forehead stopped at MacCulloch's door and rang the bell. Liz didn't need to look around to guess that some sort of drug deal was going on. It explained MacCulloch's nerves.

She was relieved when she was back in her car with the air con on, blowing the stale smell of MacCulloch's flat from her clothes. It was time to call Bernie and head back to Invergryff. Things were hotting up, and Liz wanted to make sure she was in the middle of them.

Chapter 33: Mary

It was a sports day in Scotland and for once it wasn't raining. The parents had lost their heads at this rare turn of events and families had turned up with folding chairs and coolers which the teachers only had to hope contained non-alcoholic drinks. It was officially 'taps aff' weather, no matter if the other spectators wanted it or not.

Mary would have killed for a glass of something cold. As usual, she had been in a mad rush to make it on time and had only grabbed her stuff at a run going out the door. So she had a bag-for-life to sit on and a half-melted bar of fruit and nut and that would have to do.

Sports day was in much the same vein as the Christmas nativity as far as Mary was concerned. It was too long, there were lots of kids you didn't give a crap about, but when your own child came to the front it was the best feeling ever.

This time, however, she had a knot of anxiety in her stomach. Vikki had woken up with a 'tummy ache' which signalled that her daughter hadn't got over her nerves. All Mary wanted was for Vikki to get through the day without feeling that she had embarrassed herself. Of course, if Peter could manage to finish a race without tripping up any competitors, that would be an added bonus.

The younger children had started things off and Mary enjoyed watching them attempting to at least run in the direction of the finish line. She was just beginning to relax into the day when a muscular figure appeared in her peripheral vision.

"Hello."

"Oh god, Bernie, please don't tell me you've come to have another row," Mary said. "I'm really not in the mood. Lauren's already lost one of her trainers and Johnny had a meltdown when he got tangled up in the sack race."

To her surprise, Bernie plonked herself down next to her on the mat.

"Nope. I've come to keep you company."

This had to be a Bernie Paterson trick. "What are you up to?"

"Just what I said."

They paused as the announcer yelled out another race.

"Come on, tell me what this is all about," Mary said, not enjoying the suspense.

"Jesus, can't a woman sit down where she likes these days? Look, I won't say that I felt bad about our disagreement earlier. In fact, I was impressed that you stood up to me. The wet lettuce that I met a couple of years ago wouldn't have done that."

"Oh. Thanks, I guess."

"But it played on my mind, I suppose. And Liz gave me a bollocking about my attitude, so that might have had something to do with it. But I've been thinking a lot this week about the old Bernie Paterson, the fat Bernie that didn't stand up to anyone either. And I…" Bernie shook her head. "I'm getting distracted. Look, I still think this is a stupid thing to bother with. I never went to any of Ewan's sports days."

"Of course you didn't."

Bernie held up her hand. "Let me finish, will you? I didn't go to the stupid things. But Finn went. I didn't have to go because I had a husband to send instead. And you're on your own so you don't have that option. And I guess that hadn't occurred to me up until now."

"It should have done," Mary snapped back. She wasn't quite ready to let go of her irritation towards the other woman.

"Maybe. I'm not someone who spends a lot of time worrying about other people's feelings. And to be honest, most of the time it's because I don't give a crap. But it turns out that your feelings do matter to me."

"They do?"

"Yes. Our investigative agency is considerably less efficient when you are upset."

"Ah."

They sat together and watched a group of six year olds try to trip each other up while their teacher yelled at them. Mary felt her heart lighten.

"How is Vicky doing? Still worried about her race?"

Mary shrugged. "Yeah, she's still nervous. I gave her a talk this morning. You know, the usual thing about how important it is just to take part, and how to be a good loser. Hopefully it all sunk in."

Bernie snorted. "I bloody well hope it didn't. Good loser indeed. What a load of crap."

"Right," Mary's warm fuzzy feeling was quickly evaporating.

"What did you put in her lunchbox?" Bernie asked.

"The usual. Bit of fruit, cheese and a sandwich. Trying to keep it reasonably healthy."

"You tit," Bernie replied.

Mary's mouth fell open. "What?"

"You should have filled it full of sugar. I always gave Ewan two chocolate bars and a milkshake on sports day. Big boost of sugar right before he steps up to the starting blocks. He won every time."

"Bernie that's… that's practically doping." Just when Mary thought the woman had reached her low point, Bernie could always dig her way down further.

"Yeah well, it worked, didn't it?"

Mary chewed the inside of her lip. "It really worked, did it?"

"Yep. Every time."

"Just… give me a second."

It didn't take long for Mary to find Vikki standing with a group of her pals.

"Can I have a quick word," Mary asked, pulling her daughter around the side wall of the school.

"What's up mum?"

"Nothing. Just, you know, wanted to give you a wee pep talk. And I thought you might like this." Mary pulled her emergency bar of fruit and nut out of her handbag.

"What?"

"Just thought it might be nice for you to have a wee nibble," Mary checked no one was watching as she unwrapped the bar. "Help with your nerves."

"You never let us have chocolate at school?" Vikki said, her eyes narrowed. "What's going on?"

Mary checked that no one had spotted them. "Nothing, nothing at all. Just swallow this down before the teacher arrives."

The lure of chocolate finally won over her daughter's suspicions and Vikki's wolfed down the chocolate in just a few seconds.

"Excellent. Now go out there and give them hell."

Vikki blinked. "You mean go out and try my best?"

"That's what I said."

Back at the finish line, Bernie had whipped out a blanket from nowhere and was looking quite comfortable.

"What was that all about?"

"Oh, nothing," Mary said airily. "Any news on the case?"

"Another bloody dead end," Bernie told her. "Francis got back to me about that photograph. The woman between Cammy and Gavin was Cammy's wife. Not our mystery woman at all."

"Damn," Mary said. "Well, I'm glad you came anyway. It's nice to get some recognition of how hard it can be on your own."

"I'm not sure you're going to be on your own for too much longer," Bernie replied.

Mary frowned. "What are you talking about?"

A shadow fell over them.

"Sorry I'm late," Walker said.

Chapter 34: Walker

Walker wasn't sure that adults were meant to punch the air when their kid won the sack race, but to look at Mary's face it might as well have been an Olympic medal.

"Yessss! Go Queen!" Mary yelled, breaking out into a dance of celebration. This lasted for exactly four seconds until Vikki gave her a 'you're embarrassing me' face and Mary gave her a thumbs up instead.

"I can't believe she won," his girlfriend said as she flopped back down onto the carrier bag she had been sitting on.

"She was buzzing, wasn't she," Walker said. "The way she was doing push-ups before the race started was crazy."

"Yeah, crazy. Anyway, I'm so glad you could make it."

He kissed the top of her head. "Me too. After they let Francis go, they said we could knock off early. I think Ferguson was a bit dispirited by the whole thing. He really thought he had solved the case."

"Should have listened to Bernie," Mary told him. "She's always said from the start that Francis had nothing to do with his brother's death."

"Unfortunately, we need more than just 'Bernie says so' to prove our case." Walker looked around. "Where is she anyway?" He hated it when he didn't have eyes on Paterson.

She had a habit of sneaking up on him and he was sure it wasn't good for his bloody pressure.

"She had to take a call. It was good of her to show up, considering she thinks sports day is pointless."

"Really? I thought she was into all that fitness stuff?"

"Oh, she is. She just doesn't get the point of primary school sports now that they've stopped it being so competitive. Or 'namby pamby' as she calls it. Plus she says that high intensity training is better for muscle building."

"Right."

As if saying her name had summoned her, Bernie came over to them. "How long has this got to go?"

"Only another fifteen minutes or so," Mary told her.

"Excellent. Are you free to give us a lift afterwards?"

Walker blinked. "You mean me?"

"Who else? I didn't take my car so that I could get my steps in walking over here. And Mary's car smells of wet feet and sour milk."

"Hey."

"All right," Walker agreed. Sadly, Bernie was not wrong about the smell. "I guess I'm off-duty anyway. Where do you want to go?"

"I'll tell you on the way."

Once sports day was over and they had said goodbye to the gaggle of children, Walker led the others to his car. They set off for an address in the centre of Invergryff. A drive with the WWC team in the car was never uneventful, but this time Walker almost had to stop the car when Bernie got to the bit about Liz's conversation with MacCulloch. "You're telling me that Cameron Venny owned the exact same type of car that we found Gavin's body in?"

"Yep."

"Bloody hell." Somehow Walker managed to get them to Venny's address without veering off the road. This wasn't made any easier by the fact that Mary had to have her disco mix on whenever they were in the car.

"We needed a soundtrack," Mary told him as he turned off the engine. "And I think that the disco tunes of the nineties are fitting."

"It's just a little hard to concentrate on clearing up a wrongful death with *Love Shack* blaring out of the speakers," Walker said.

"For once I agree with the copper," Bernie said. "Now which one of those flats is Venny's?"

The three of them got out of the car and looked around. The crisp white render had been newly applied to brighten up the block of flats, but it still had the bones of sixties brutalism underneath. Following an unspoken rule, someone had left a discarded mattress next to the main door.

"It says on the system flat seven, building C."

"All right then, let's go."

Bernie took a step forward, but Walker blocked her path.

"Just where do you think you're going."

"Off to have a wee chat with Cameron Venny," Bernie snapped. "You can hold our handbags for us if you like."

Walker was getting one of his 'Bernie headaches'. "I haven't even spoken to the office yet."

"You do that and get a load of squad cars over and you won't see Venny for dust. He's a career criminal, you know. A hint of a siren and he'll be out of here."

"Let me at least check on the car first," Walker suggested.

Bernie pursed her lips, but that was as close to assent as he was going to get.

Walker pulled out his phone and called McNicholl on her mobile.

"What's up?"

"Just a quick question. Can I just check with you about the car that was used to dump Gavin Eyre's body? Has there been any news on tracing it?"

"Hang on a sec, let me check." Walker could hear her fingers clacking on the keys while he waited. "Nah, nothing new. Stolen in ninety-three, but after that nothing until it turned up in the water."

"You don't know when it ended up in the reservoir?"

"No way of telling, sadly."

Walker hesitated, then said. "I'm going to follow up on a lead. It's a bit… out there, but if it comes good then I'll call it in. Can you mark me down as officially on-duty?"

There was a long pause before she answered. "I don't know what you're up to, but if it's going to get us a breakthrough on this case then go ahead. But if it all turns to crap, I knew nothing about it," McNicholl added.

He hung up the phone and turned around to face Bernie and Mary.

"That car that was given to Cammy, you're sure it was a red Escort?"

"Yes."

"All right. We'll go and speak to him."

Bernie cleared her throat. "I was thinking we would speak to him alone."

"What?"

"It's our lead after all. You're just the chauffeur."

Walker bit down on an angry reply. The weather had decided to join in the drama by pelting down big drops of rain that ran down his neck.

"Let's at least go and stand in the stairwell," Mary said. "I didn't bring a brolly."

They huddled under the overhanging roof in a small space that brought him uncomfortably close to a scowling Bernie.

"I know you think I'm being difficult," Walker told her, "but there are procedures that we need to follow. We can't do anything that would prevent us from bringing Gavin's killer to justice."

"You wouldn't even have the right suspect if it wasn't for us. You've only just released Francis Eyre."

"How did you know that?"

"He texted me."

"Of course he did."

Bernie sighed. "Here's the thing, I spoke to Francis right after you let him out of jail."

"You mean after he was released from the police station," Walker said wearily. "There was no jail involved."

"Whatever. I asked him about this woman that we know Gavin was shagging at the care home. At first he said he didn't know anything, but I kept pushing. Then he said that Gavin might have mentioned once that he was seeing someone who was married."

"Married?"

"That's right. Gavin sort of shrugged it off, and Francis reckoned at the time that he was making it up. Trying to sound like he was a player or something. But what if he was telling the truth?"

Mary's eyes glittered with excitement. "It's all coming together, isn't it. What if Cammy's wife was the one that Gavin was shagging? There's your motive."

Walker had to admit it all sounded plausible.

"Let us go and talk to Cammy," Bernie repeated. "You know what the man is like. He's been interviewed by the police more times than Mary's had empire biscuits. You go in there and it'll be all 'no comment' and 'where's my lawyer'. Let us have a go."

"No," Walker replied.

"It's not a bad idea," Mary said.

Walker rubbed at his chin. "It might just be the worst idea that anyone has ever had. Ever."

"Look, you said yourself this case is a nightmare," Bernie told him. "All the evidence disappeared thirty years ago. The only way you're going to get anywhere is with a confession."

"And you reckon you can walk in there and get him to confess?"

"That's right."

It must be nice to have the confidence of a Bernadette Paterson, Walker thought. The sort of self-belief that you could throw rocks at. And the thing was, more often than not she turned out to be right. But was it worth staking his career on it?

"You've got five minutes. And if anything happens to Mary –"

"You'll throw me in the reservoir," Bernie nodded. "I get it."

"Love you," Mary said, pressing her lips to his then skipping up the stairs like she was a kid going on an adventure.

Five minutes, Walker told himself, checking his watch. Just five minutes. He knew they would be the longest of his life.

Chapter 35: Bernie

"I can't believe Walker let you come up here with me," Bernie said as she and Mary climbed the stairs.

"We had a little chat about my work and how it's just as important as his," Mary explained. "Plus I reckon he knows I can take care of myself.

"Could be. Or alternatively, he could be calling it into the station right now," Bernie replied.

"Yeah. Maybe we should walk a bit faster?"

Bernie didn't need telling. Seven sets of stairs would take them up to Cammy Venny's flat and she hadn't spent the last three decades of her life in the gym for nothing. By the time she was ringing his doorbell, Mary was a flight below and making noises like a wounded walrus.

Cammy's eyes bulged when he saw who was standing in front of him, but Bernie's patented foot-in-door technique prevented him from slamming it in her face.

"Hello. Not at the bowling club today?"

"It's my day off," Cammy said. "Why are you here?"

"Oh, we just wanted to have a little word. Plus my friend Mary here looks like she needs a glass of water. You wouldn't leave a lady on the stairs to have a heart attack, would you?"

Cammy twitched a shoulder and stood aside to let them in.

"I'm not having a heart attack," Mary puffed as she went through the doorway. "I just need a wee sit down."

Although small, Venny's flat was neat and tidy, unlike most of the places they'd been recently. Mary flopped down onto the sofa and started fanning herself with her hand.

"You need to do some exercise," Bernie told her.

Mary just glared at her.

Cammy appeared from the kitchen which was through an archway from the living room and handed her a glass of water.

"Thank you so much," Mary beamed at him. "You're a lifesaver."

Bernie looked around the room while the host's attention was distracted. It was a typical bachelor pad, the only furniture being a sofa, a table and a large television. There was a mantelpiece above a gas fire with four pictures in frames. Each of them was of Cammy and his wife.

She turned back to Mary who caught her eye and tilted her neck in what the woman probably thought was a subtle gesture towards the photographs.

"You should have another drink," Cammy told her. "You've started twitching."

While an embarrassed Mary drank her water, Bernie tried to think of how to start the conversation about Gavin Eyre. And then she remembered that subtlety never got her anywhere.

"How old was your wife when she died?" Bernie asked, pointing at the photograph of the happy couple on their wedding day.

"She was twenty-eight."

"That would have been what, June ninety-four?"

"May."

"So only a few weeks after Gavin Eyre disappeared."

"Guess so." Cammy dropped his eyes and it was all Bernie could do not to scream 'Gotcha!'.

"It must have been a shock for her. To get a terminal diagnosis so young," Bernie explained. "I was a nurse in a care home, so I've seen my fair share of bad news."

Cammy pulled out his vape pen and started passing it between his hands. "It was bloody awful. When they told her she was sick, they said she might last a year. She was dead in two months."

"Aye, it happens like that sometimes."

"You must have loved her very much," Mary said. "To still keep her photos up after all these years."

"She was my wife," Cammy replied.

"Did you let her drive your wee red Ford," Bernie asked him. "The one that the police pulled out of the reservoir."

This time, Cammy raised his head and looked at her, realisation dawning.

"Oh," he said. "I thought maybe someone would work that out."

And just like that, Cammy began his confession. Somehow Bernie had thought it would be more difficult than that, but the man seemed to want to get the words out.

"It should never have happened," Cammy said, taking a puff of his vape. "I caught them at it, right in the act, in our home, can you imagine? And then she told me it was a one-off. But I knew they were still meeting up, they had just found somewhere else to do it."

"When did you realise that your wife was sleeping with Gavin Eyre?" Bernie asked.

"It wasn't her fault," Cameron said quietly, as if it was something he had told himself before. "She was vulnerable! She had just been told she had months to live. He took advantage of her."

Bernie didn't reply to this one. The truth was, in her job as a nurse she had seen plenty of people given the sort of terrible news that Cammy's wife had received. And yes, maybe it did make them vulnerable. But sometimes it made them determined to live life to the fullest. Gavin Eyre might have taken advantage, or Jen Venny might have known exactly what she was doing. With both of them dead, no one would ever know for sure.

"When did you decide to do something about it?"

"When I realised it wasn't stopping. That she… And then I saw him come out of the pub that night. Half-cut, staggering along the road, not a care in the bloody world. And all I could think was: this arsehole is going to go on living long after my Jen is dead. And I just couldn't bear it any more."

He took a deep breath. "Honestly, I thought they would find him not long after I dumped the body. They were meant to drain the reservoir years ago. But they never did."

"Budget cuts," Bernie tutted.

"Yeah," Cammy sniffed. "Budget cuts."

There was a thump at the door. Bernie assumed Walker had got fed up of waiting.

"I better let him in," Mary said, clearly thinking the same thing. She pulled the door open only to be pushed aside by a large figure holding a knife.

"Is that the bastard that killed my brother?" Francis Eyre asked.

"Oh bloody hell," Bernie said. "This is not a good time, all right?"

Francis ignored her, pushing past so that Cammy was up against the back wall with no one to save him from the ball of rage in front of him.

"You left him to rot," Francis said and Bernie noted his hand was shaking as he pointed the knife at Cammy's chest.

The room fell into a dangerous silence.

"Personally, I don't care if you do kill him," Bernie said with a shrug.

"Bernie!" Mary's shocked voice rang out across the room.

Francis looked at them as if looking for the catch.

"Go on, if you're going to do it, I do hope you'll be quick. I've got a dumbells class at six."

He took another step towards Cammy who was quaking in fear.

"Unless," Bernie held up her index finger, "you might just want to think about it for a minute. Yes, you could murder the cowardly scumbag who killed your brother. Not a person in this room would blame you for it. Probably not even the unfortunate Mr Venny himself. But what about the person no one thinks about? The real victim here."

Francis's brow creased in confusion.

"Kids!" Bernie laughed. "So ungrateful. Even with me giving you clues you're still not thinking of your mother."

"My mother? What the hell has she got to do with this?"

Bernie stepped forward so that she was only an inch from the man's face, standing in between the two men. "That woman has spent thirty years mourning the death of one son. Do you really think I'm going to let her spend the next thirty years mourning the other one in prison? No, sonny, not on my watch."

She lifted her right knee in a well-rehearsed movement.

Francis made a tiny 'oof' sound and toppled backwards, just as Bernie grabbed the knife out of his hand.

"Never fails," Bernie said, her hands on her hips.

Mary picked up her phone and Bernie could hear her calling Walker. Cammy had collapsed in the corner and was quietly weeping to himself. Francis was still gasping for air, but she made sure that there was nothing near him he could use as a weapon and put her hiking boot on his back just for insurance.

Bernie grinned. Just another day in the life of the Wronged Women's Co-operative. But this had been a bloody good one.

Epilogue

"If I have another peach schnapps then I'm going to be sick," Liz said as she sat back down at the table. The speakers above her head were pumping out music that was a good few decibels too loud and the reflections from the glitterball were hurting her eyes.

"We've only been here for an hour," Bernie told her. "You're turning into a lightweight."

"I haven't been on a proper night out since Isioma was born," Liz replied. "My alcohol tolerance is pretty much non-existent."

Bernie, who was the sort of person that could drink gin for a week solid and not get a hangover, grabbed another cocktail.

"Come on, we're celebrating! It's about time we had a night out."

"It's four o'clock in the afternoon," Liz reminded her. "I don't think this counts as a night out."

"Apparently it's the new thing; clubbing for the over forties. Get your glad rags on, drink like your twenty again then home and tucked up in bed by nine."

When Bernie had invited her to the 'Remember the Nineties' afternoon it had seemed like fate. So much of their most recent case had been based in the heady days of Liz's teens.

And although it might be a bit loud and garish for a time when the sun was still up, even Liz had to admit it was a good laugh.

"I do love a bit of NSYNC," Liz said as the adolescent voices blared out above her head.

"I was always more of a Backstreet Boys girl," Bernie told her. "Shall I get us another drink?"

"Not yet," Liz pleaded. "Let my stomach recover. It's not the alcohol that gets you, it's the sugar."

"True," Bernie laughed. They watched the people around them for a few minutes in silence.

"There's something I haven't quite worked out about what happened with Cammy yesterday," Liz said, determined to get something off her mind that had been bothering her all day.

"Really? What?"

"According to Mary you said you didn't tell Francis Eyre about Cammy being the killer. That he worked it all out by himself and just happened to turn up at the right moment."

"That's right."

"You're a dreadful liar."

Bernie winked. "I told her what she wanted to hear. Besides, that hulking boyfriend of hers was hanging around and I knew that he would get all judgy about it."

"That could all have gone very wrong, Berns, you know that."

"I had everything under control."

Liz pressed her lips together.

"Look, Cammy was a broken man. I could tell that from the minute I set eyes on him. You used to get men like that in the care home all the time. Their wife died and it just hollowed out their life, leaving them with nothing. That was Cameron Venny. Sure, when she was still alive he was angry enough to kill the man that might take her away. But after she was dead, the fire was out of him. We were never in any danger."

"And what about Francis?" Liz said, not willing to give up the point. "He was a dangerous guy."

"Not for us," Bernie said with a shrug. "He only wanted his brother's killer."

"I still think it was a risk."

"Nah," Bernie grinned. "This blue eyeshadow is a risk."

Liz stared at her for a moment, then burst out laughing. "God, you're a bloody nightmare Bernadette Paterson."

"I know," Bernie said. "It is nice to relive the nineties though. Or at least the good bits of it."

"Yeah."

The DJ changed the tune and the whole room started to 'Vogue'.

"Oh, we've got to dance," Bernie said, getting to her feet. "Madonna is my spirit animal."

"I'm not sure I'm up for a dance," Liz replied.

"Come on, I would never have got up and danced back in my chunky days. I want a boogie." She grabbed Liz's hand and dragged her over to the dance floor where a group of women were already jigging around like they were on MTV.

The dancefloor was crowded but full of laughter and joy and middle-aged women letting loose. Despite herself, Liz was joining in and actually having a good time.

"Why isn't Mary here?" Bernie shouted over the top of the synthesizers and electric guitars.

Liz shrugged. "She said she had something to do."

"Probably hanging out with that handsome boyfriend of hers."

"Probably."

■■

The curtains had been opened in Mrs Eyre's living room, but it still had the forgotten, stuffy air that Mary remembered from the first time she visited.

"Sorry to pop in again," she said as Mrs Eyre led her into the familiar living room. "It's nothing urgent, just a few things to clear up so I can finish my paperwork."

"Bargain Hunt is just about to start," Mrs Eyre said, gesturing to the sofa.

Mary smiled. "Fancy that," she said, as if she hadn't timed it to the minute. She sat down on the other end of the sofa and watched as the presenter introduced the two couples playing today, who for some unknown reason all seemed to be orthodontists.

"Francis came over earlier," Mrs Eyre told her.

"Oh yes?"

"He wanted to check I was all right. First time he'd been around in months."

"Maybe he'll come over more often now," Mary suggested.

"Maybe."

"The police told you about Cameron Venny, did they?" Mary said and Mrs Eyre nodded in confirmation.

"I don't know if I mentioned before, but my other half is a police officer."

Mrs Eyre shook her head.

"He was telling me about the interview they did with Venny back at the station. He's given a full confession, by the way, so you don't need to worry about that."

"That's good."

"There was one weird thing though," Mary said, her eyes

flicking to the woman next to her, "Venny told the police that he killed Gavin as he was walking home from the pub. And the thing is, you said you saw him that night. But I don't think you did, did you? If I've got the timings right, then he was already dead by then."

Mrs Eyre blinked back tears. "You're very clever, aren't you?"

"It's my job," Mary said. "It's a bit of a curse really. That and the inability to leave any loose ends alone. I suppose I wanted to understand why you lied. I know you weren't involved in his death, and neither was Francis. So why didn't you tell the truth?"

"I should have seen him before he died," Mrs Eyre said, her head dropping low. "But we'd had a dreadful row earlier that day. I had a friend at the care home, one of the cleaners. And she told me that he'd been using it to... well, you know all about that. He'd always had an eye for the ladies, my Gavin. And no sense, of course, which was the problem. I thought he was going to lose his job, so before he went to the pub I had a go at him. It got heated, he said things, I said things... And you can't take it back, can you? Not when they're dead."

"No, you can't."

"When he disappeared I thought after we had the row he went out and... and he killed himself. He had asked about his dad, you see. And I thought he couldn't bear to have a mother that had... done what was necessary. I thought he had thrown himself in the river and they never found his body."

Mary sucked in a breath. "You blamed yourself for all these

years."

"Of course I bloody well did."

"But now you know that you weren't to blame."

Mrs Eyre sniffed. "You think I shouldn't feel guilty anymore? If I hadn't lied about when I last saw him they might have caught his killer years ago."

Mary didn't have an answer for that one. On the screen, two women were arguing over an ugly red and yellow vase.

"If that's Clarice Cliff then I'm a silver tea set," Mary said.

"Aye, it's probably got Made in China written on the bottom," Mrs Eyre said and they both laughed.

"I suppose you'll be rushing off soon," Mrs Eyre said. On the telly the auction had started and the people in cheap fleeces were already bemoaning their losses.

"Nah. It's a double episode," Mary replied. "Mind if I stick around for a bit?"

"Sure," Mrs Eyre replied. "I might even have a box of chocolate biscuits from Christmas if you fancy one?"

"That would be perfect."

Afterword

Thank you for reading *Body of Water*. The idea for this novel came to me when they drained a reservoir near where I live in Paisley, the basis for the fictional town of Invergryff. Half a dozen cars were found in the mud once all the water had drained, all from the nineties. In Paisley, however, there were no bodies in the water – real life has no sense of narrative – but the seed had been sown.

And for a lady of my era a little bit of nineties nostalgia is always welcome. I might not be able to fit into my bootcut jeans anymore, but my love for cheesy boy bands and blue eyeshadow will never die.

If you'd like to continue reading this series, book ten is available to order now!

Printed in Great Britain
by Amazon